Diary of a Fortnite Noob

ALSO BY AJ DIAZ

THE TAYLOR KELSEY MYSTERY SERIES
Mystery of the 19th Hole
Mystery of the 101st Meter
Mystery of the 33rd Chess Piece
Mystery of the 51st Star
Mystery of the 13th Floor
Mystery of the 25th Hour
Mystery of the Second Name

MINECRAFT NOVELS w/ Jake Turner
Herobrine In Real Life
Minecraft High School
Fright Night: Minecraft High School Book 2

STEAMPUNK SERIES
The Girl With The Train
The Ostentatious Tale of a Third-Rate Smuggler

Follow AJ on Social Media.
Instagram: @theAJDiaz
Twitter: @theAJDiaz
Facebook: @theAJDiaz

Diary of a Fortnite Noob
An Unofficial Fortnite Adventure

by

AJ Diaz

For A FREE Minecraft Novel
Visit theAJDiaz.com/Minecraft

To Allen and Julie.
Your lives turned out inexplicably different from what you had planned.
But they turned out far better in ways you never could have imagined.
Thank you for everything.

A Meteor Destroys My School

1

I ran out of my house, the screen door slamming back against the frame. My eyes were filled with tears and I wanted to sob but I held it back as best as I could. My mom was at the door, opening the screen and yelling to me, "Allen, come back!"

No way.

There was no way I was going back there.

She watched me from the door as I ran down our short front yard and banked right, taking off down the street.

When I was out of her sight, hidden in a shadow because it was late at night and the sun was long gone, I turned back and watched, waiting. She didn't come out of the house.

I sat on the curb, in the mostly dark, crying into my hands.

The tears were dripping all around my fingers, falling onto the asphalt.

I didn't care if anyone saw me.

I wasn't really paying attention to anyone else.

It was late and cold and I was tired and sad and nothing could ever get worse than what was happening to me right now.

I was only nine-years-old at the time.

Looking back, it still makes my eyes teary-eyed.

I had so much to learn.

I'm fourteen now, and I'm sure I still have so much to learn, but before I get to where I'm at now, I need to tell you about that night when I was nine.

My parents had just sat me down in our small living room. I'd sat at the fireplace. It wasn't on. They'd sat on the couch and explained that they were getting divorced.

I'd known that they fought a lot.

But I hadn't expected them to get divorced.

It crushed me.

I was just a kid.

Do you know how it feels?

Maybe you do. Maybe you don't.

It feels as if someone punched you really hard and took all the air out of your body. I couldn't stop crying because I kept asking myself this question: My parents said that they loved each other. They'd told each other that on their wedding day. They'd put rings on each other's fingers and they'd promised they'd stay together. If they said they'd loved each other and then got divorced that meant they were lying. And it made me question whether or not they actually loved me.

How could they say they loved each other and yet get divorced?

How could they say they loved me and get divorced, hurting my feelings so much?

I had so many emotions inside me that I didn't know what to do. I felt crushed and I could hardly breathe. I wanted to shout at the sky and say bad words. I might have said a few under my breath, because how could my parents do such a thing?

They said they loved each other and yet they didn't because they were getting a divorce, and I wondered what that meant for me. *Did they even really love me?*

Sure, they'd fought a lot.

But we'd had so many great times.

All I knew is that I would never do that to my kids. EVER.

"Kid, are you okay?" someone said from across the street.

It made me jump because I'd nearly forgotten I was in the middle of a street. Looking up and trying to wipe my eyes with my already soaked hands, I saw an older-looking gentleman with white hair. He looked like he could be a doctor or a professor of some kind. He was wearing a sweater vest and was walking his dog, which was a small fluffy white dog that looked really happy.

The man started walking across the street towards me.

I wiped my eyes with my shirt.

Then the dog was next to me, licking at my face. I was really sad, but the dog helped a little. I pet it and looked up at the man.

"Son," he said, sounding very nice and concerned. "Are you okay?"

"Yeah," I said.

The man just stood there, watching me pet the dog. "His name is Thor."

"Like from '*Adventures in Babysitting*?'" I said.

"That's right."

"That's cool," I said. "Who's a good dog?" I said. The dog was licking my cheek and it tickled, making me laugh.

The nice man leaned down on a knee next to me, petting the dog as well. "He likes you."

"Yeah, he's a good Thor."

"What's your name?" the man asked.

"Allen. Allen Diaz."

"What do you want to do with your life, Allen?"

I thought about it, sniffling, cuddling my head against Thor's. "I'm not sure yet. But probably I want to become a gymnast or a martial artist like Bruce Lee, or maybe even an artist like my dad."

"Do you do all of those things?"

"Yes, sir. Everyday. I practice hard. My mom says I have a lot of talents. My dad is very talented so that's probably where I get it from."

"Well, that's good. It sounds like you have a lot of talents."

"I'm also pretty good at dancing. I'm learning how to breakdance. My friends in middle-school are already in competitions and they're making money from it. Of course, it's mostly a fun thing for me. I might become a martial artist and own my own dojo. Or become a gymnastics coach after I'm done doing it myself, and maybe even coach people in the Olympics. That would be cool. My friend's dad is a contractor. He makes a lot of money. Maybe I'll try that one day."

"You certainly have a lot of dreams, don't you, Allen?"

"Yes, sir."

The man tilted up my head by touching my chin. He looked into my eyes and suddenly lots of my negative emotions went away. I felt safe for the moment. He had old guy eyes—eyes that made me feel calm inside, kind of.

"Listen carefully to me, Allen. Never let go of your dreams. Never, ever, ever, ever, give up. I think you'll become a great martial artist and gymnast and you'll do all kinds of flips and even be a breakdancer too. Maybe even a contractor who makes lots of money. You know why I think that?"

I didn't. But it felt really good that an adult was saying he believed in me. My dad never told me things like this.

I shook my head.

"I can tell," the man said. "Some people—I can tell that they'll never make it. Because they think too small, and they don't dream. And they don't believe in themselves. But you, Allen, you do. You may forget it, but try not to, son. Because you're special."

After he said that, he rubbed my head, messing up my hair, and stood up. "It was nice meeting you. Thor and I have to finish our walk now and go to bed. And you probably should too."

"Nice meeting you, sir," I said, standing up as well.

I watched the old man and Thor walk down the street.

The further they got, the more all the sad feelings were coming back to me about my parents. I started walking home anyway. I had to go back at some point.

When I finally got home, I realized I didn't want to go

back in.

I just couldn't handle it.

So instead I walked to the side of the house, climbed up the fence and climbed from the top of the fence onto the roof. A lot of times, during the day, I would stand on top of the fence—which was pretty high—and practice all of my martial arts kicks, practicing my balance.

Right now, practicing kicks was the last thing on my mind.

I climbed up to the top of my roof and sat there on the tiles, under the moonlight, looking at the sky, and tears started streaming down my face once more.

I was remembering all the good times I'd had with my parents, and I knew in my heart that they were ruining everything, and I felt hopeless. Because there was nothing at all I could do about it.

I wondered if it was my fault.

I started thinking of all the times I'd disobeyed them and gotten into trouble, all the times I'd caused them to fight because they disagreed on how they should punish me.

What could I do?

I was just a kid.

I sat on the roof for a long time. I quickly forgot about Thor and the old man and I simply cried. Finally, after a long time, my tears dried up and I felt like I didn't really have any left. I looked up into the sky, at the moon and the stars.

I started thinking about aliens and how there must be aliens up there. I'd seen *Star Wars* and a lot of space movies, and there just had to be life on other planets.

Looking up at the stars, I knew one thing. I didn't want

to be on Earth anymore. I wanted to be up there, away from all of my problems. Away from all the pain in my heart.

If I was truly special, then the aliens would surely take me.

Looking up, I shouted, "Take me! If you're up there, take me!"

I waited.

There was no response.

"Please take me," I said, not as loud. "Please," I whispered.

I watched and waited for many long seconds.

When nothing happened, I hung my head.

Which is when something happened—something crazy.

I saw it out of the corner of my eye. A light in the sky. Looking up from my forlorn pose, I saw it in the sky—a meteor. It was bright and big and flying down from high overhead. It was flaming, casting a giant orange glow, even onto my skin.

I wondered if it actually was aliens.

As time passed, I realized it was just a meteor.

But it was a big meteor and it was coming right down towards my town!

That, ladies and gentlemen, is where our story begins.

See, this story is a crazy one, and it's a true one. But it all started that night that my parents told me they were getting divorced, because that night I sat on the roof and watched the meteor crash land. It landed a few blocks away from my house, right on top of my school—which was also connected to the middle-school and high school I would end up going to. It obliterated the school, wrecked it, tore it to pieces.

And ever since that day, ever since that day the meteor destroyed the schools, our small town was never the same. Weird things started happening. Really weird things.

2

When the meteor hit the ground, the entire Earth shook from side to side and I had to lay down flat on the roof to make sure I didn't get thrown off. That's how intense it was!

I whipped out my flip phone from my pocket and texted my three main friends at the time to get on their bikes and skates and scooters and meet me at our school, where the meteor had landed.

Then I was climbing down from the roof.

I threw open our garage door and got my bike.

That's when my mom came into the garage. "Honey, are you okay?"

"Yeah, Mom, gotta go."

"No, it's too dangerous."

But I was already on my bike, riding away.

"Allen, come back!" she yelled.

I didn't listen.

I was riding down our street as fast as I could. I could feel my phone vibrating in my pocket, which meant that my friends were texting back that they were on their way. I knew they'd come. They were legit.

My school was only seven minutes away, and I was pedaling hard. I would probably get there first.

As I got within a few streets of my school, I could see tall flames going up towards the sky, spewing thick smoke into the atmosphere. It was crazy! I was breathing in the smoke and it was kinda hard to breathe. I wondered if aliens had come down with the meteor. I hoped they had. And I hoped they were friendly.

When I got two streets away I saw two of my friends riding their bikes towards me. I pulled up and waited for them. It was Kyle and Nick.

"Allen!" one of them yelled. "Did it destroy our school?"

"I think it did."

Then we were all riding together. We saw some adults coming out of their houses and yelling at us, "Crazy kids! Don't go towards the fire!"

We didn't care.

We needed to see this first-hand.

Finally we pulled onto the street and we could see gigantic flames—bigger than I'd ever seen before or since —licking upwards from the crumbled bricks of all three schools: our elementary school, and our future middle-school and high schools.

"Yes!" said Kyle.

We looked at him.

"No school tomorrow," he said. "We should totally play *TimeSplitters* all day tomorrow at my house."

"I"ll bring turkey jerky," said Nick.

"I"ll bring brownies," I said, but mostly I was watching the flames around the schools. I could see a giant chunk of rock from the meteor. It was flaming and red-hot.

Then we didn't say much about our next day's plans. Instead, we biked around the schools, viewing the fire from all the angles. Firemen by the dozens were showing up now, announced by flashing lights and ear-killing sirens. Firemen kept yelling at us to leave, but we kept biking away from them, watching everything unfold.

Finally, some policemen drove up to us and told us to leave.

We went a street back and watched the firemen put out the fires, or try to put out the fires.

"Sick," said Nick.

"Insane," said Kyle.

"Crazy," I said.

"I wonder if we're going to get radioactive powers," said Kyle. "Or if the spiders that lived in the school are going to get radioactive powers and turn giant and eat all the adults in the town."

"That would be sick," said Nick. "Like a horror movie."

"What if there are aliens in there?" I said. "And they have a spaceship somewhere."

"Sick," said Nick. "But what if the aliens kill us all?"

"Maybe they're nice aliens. Why do people always think aliens want to kill us?"

"Well, why else would aliens come here if not to harvest our resources?" said Kyle.

"I suppose," I said.

"Sick," said Nick.

But none of those things happened. What happened was even stranger and less expected. Keep reading...

3

We got a new principal.

That's how things got weird after the meteor crash. Nothing radioactive happened as far as we could tell. Instead, a billionaire named Nicolas Petrov purchased all three schools in our neighborhood and became the principal of all three. I didn't know it was possible to be a principal of all the schools. Since he was a billionaire he had the schools rebuilt in record time—one week. We'd been sure we would have gotten school off for at least a month or two but then stupid Petrov showed up.

He was, like, Russian or something, and had a thick accent.

He'd had the schools rebuilt according to his own designs.

And he had some wild design ideas.

For example, he built a giant fake rocket ship on top of the auditorium building. Each section of the school was a different theme, kind of like a theme park. The cafeteria was a space station. All the fountains in the school were edible chocolate fountains. All the buildings were colorful and everyone was mandated to have a favorite color. Seriously. You had to have a favorite color.

To be honest, we all loved Petrov, other than the fact that he'd rebuilt our schools in record time. He wasn't always around because he was busy being a billionaire. He left a lot of people in charge though, and we all suspected that they were *animatrons*—like, robots. Because they were super weird. But whatever.

The schools were actually pretty cool.

That's a gross thing to admit—that school is cool.

But they kinda were.

There were entire rides and there was even a ride that took you up on a track up above the school and you got to overlook the city. It was slow-moving and really cool. Some of the high school boys would try to take girls up on it to make out (gross), but the robots—teachers and school faculty staff—wouldn't let them. That was the other reason we thought the faculty were robots. They were too smart and always caught everyone before they did anything bad. But they were stupid at the same time.

Here's an example.

Last week, I was taking a bite of a candy apple that I'd won from cashing in all my tickets from the arcade that Petrov had installed. I was about to take a big bite of it when one of the robots, a male wearing a candy striper outfit—because he worked at the Candy Shack (a booth in our school's Candy Emporium)—grabbed the apple from my hand and said, "If you were to take another bite you would have chipped your tooth."

"What?" I said. "That's crazy. My teeth are in perfect condition."

"But there is a spec in this apple, sir," said the man—errrr, robot.

The man pulled out a piece of plastic from the apple and held it up. "See what I mean? You would have surely died, young man."

"I would have lived," I said. "I only would have chipped my tooth at worst and even that would have been unlikely."

"Do not doubt me, sir. It is a gigantic piece of plastic, as you can see."

"It's not that big."

"Oh, it is, sir."

"No it isn't," I said, reaching for my candy apple.

The man didn't let me have the apple back. "You can have it back on one condition," he said. "That you promise me you will never chip your tooth on plastic or metal or on any hardened substance."

"Sure," I said.

"And don't do drugs," he said.

"I won't."

"Except if the dentist or your doctor allows it for surgical or pain-related purposes."

"Fine."

"Do you agree?"

"Yes."

"Are you sure?"

"Yes." I was getting annoyed and wanted my candy apple back.

Finally, he handed it back to me.

Then, when he didn't think I was looking, he dropped the piece of plastic in his mouth and swallowed it.

"Pleasant conversation, young man," he said, patting me on the head. Then he rolled away on his skates. Oh, yeah, did I mention that all of the faculty, including all of our teachers, wore skates 24/7? And they skated everywhere. We were encouraged to wear skates as much as possible.

We did.

And we were all pretty good at skating.

If that's not robot behavior, the kind exhibited in the situation I just explained, then I don't know what is.

Anyway, this whole story begins a few years after the meteor struck our town. Now. I'm fourteen-years-old. We were two-and-a-half months into high school when it happened.

And it all started when I nearly made a complete idiot out of myself in front of the prettiest girl in school. Her name was Julie.

4

After my parents divorced, my mom moved away, out of state, and I ended up staying with my dad. He was fine, most of the time, except when he was drunk. Which is when he got terribly angry.

Like tonight.

I got home late from hanging out at the mall and when I stepped through my front door, he yelled, "Allen! You were supposed to mow the lawn today!" And then he said a bunch of cuss words. He was yelling from his room, didn't see me yet.

I ran across the living room, down the hall, into my room, shut my door and locked it. I started throwing open my dresser drawers and selecting an outfit for the following day. I packed them in my school backpack along with my books and my phone charger.

Then I heard my drunken dad coming down the hall, yelling all the way down, heavy footsteps. He was ready for a fight. He yelled a lot, always when he was drunk. Always at me or the next-door neighbors who had called the police on him a few times because he gets so loud.

I've learned that it's best for me to just get out of the house.

Now he was banging on my door.

"Open up, kid!" he was yelling.

I threw open my window, climbed out, and took off running down the street.

I went where I always went. To my friend Dev's house. My friend Dev is a funny guy. We met and became best friends in seventh grade. Everyday he showed up to school wearing the same ratty, tattered, gross clothes. He always wore the same dirty hat. He never smelled, so he must have washed the clothes everyday, but he just looked gross.

Everyone thought he was weird and no one really hung out with him. I would always see him alone and started to feel bad for him so I went over to his table at lunch and talked to him. He was actually really friendly and cool. I was shocked. He was playing 'Flappy Bird' on his iPad.

Okay. So he wasn't *that* cool.

Anyway, we started hanging at school. I liked him because he was super smart. He liked to program and code on computers. He loved eighties movies and got all my references. He was a nerd. But he was a cool nerd.

And there aren't many of those.

I already had had a lot of friends. I was the one guy who was friends with all the different groups in our school —the skaters, the jocks, cheerleaders (those ones were my favorite), the tweakers, the losers, the goths, the mods, everyone.

But Dev was just so chill I couldn't help but want to hang out with him.

And because he hanged out with me, he started making a lot more friends.

The weird thing was he would never invite me to his house.

So one day I invited myself.

I went over one evening and our plan was to play video games. When I pulled up to his address, I thought I was at the wrong place. He lived in a freakin' mansion!

His parents were rich programmers, and he hadn't told anyone.

His bedroom was the size of my house. He even had butlers. He had a butler named Jefferson whose family had been serving his family for generations. Apparently, his dad's family had come from riches. They'd worked in manufacturing.

Dev loved his name because the word "dev" is short for "developer"—as in, computer programmer. And Dev, like his parents, loved making apps and games for phones and computers. Dev had built ten apps on the app store and made twenty thousand dollars a month for himself.

Being in his room, I saw what he spent it on.

He had every game system under the sun, from the first systems—like Atari, Sega, Nintendo—to Xbox ONE and PS4. He owned thousands of video games. He owned a bunch of dirt bikes that he never rode but that he kept in his room. He owned a few old-fashioned Camaro's that he kept in a garage his parents gave him on one side of the property. His property had tennis courts, basketball courts, and multiple pools. He even had a hot sister in her twenties that I saw by the pool one time. Which was great.

"What the heck, bro," I'd told him. "Why didn't you tell me you were rich?" I'd said when I was standing in his room that first time.

He only shrugged.

"Why do you wear such stupid clothes?" I'd asked.

He shrugged.

"Is there a reason?"

"I don't have time for fashion," he'd said.

That day, I took him to the mall, took his debit card (because he was loaded), and we bought up the mall for him. We bought him so many clothes I was a little jealous. He did buy me a few new pairs of jeans as compensation for helping him with his fashion.

I had him looking like a stud.

The next day at school, two girls flirted with him.

Oh yeah, I'd bought him hair gel.

We'd been best friends ever since.

That night, I ran away from my dad to Dev's. Dev showed me a way I could hop his fence and avoid the cameras. The guard dogs already knew my scent and knew I was a friend, so they ran over to me and licked me. Two great big German Shepherds. I snuck around to the back of the mansion and climbed up to Dev's window. I'd told him about how my dad got crazy when he was drunk, so Dev always left his window open for me.

I climbed in and saw him in his typical place, in his PewDiePie gaming chair, before a wall of TVs. Yeah, he had a wall with ten televisions on it. It was OP.

He was playing *Fortnite* and I heard him yelling into his headset: "Get the dub! Get the dub! Get the freakin' dub!"

Then he sighed as if he'd lost.

He had.

He took off his headset. "Hey, Allen. You should play. Let's squad up."

"I've never played. Besides, I suck at video games."

"Yeah, but you're so good at everything else," he said. "You're the only person I know who can beat me at chess and, at the same time, you're an expert martial artist and gymnast."

He was right. I could do a double backflip.

I could do any kind of flip, really.

I'd gotten in a few fights in eighth grade. One time four guys tried to jump me at once. I beat them all up. No sweat. (Okay, a little bit of sweat. But still.)

"I'm a noob, bro," I said.

"You're a *Fortnite* noob, but I think you're such a talented person your talents will transfer over."

Dev had set up a corner of his room into a small gym for me to practice parkour and do my workouts while he gamed and coded.

"If I don't keep practicing my stuff, I'll lose my skills."

"Just play one game," he said.

"Nah," I said.

I took off my sweatshirt so that I was wearing a tank-top. I jumped onto the pull-up bar and busted out a quick twenty-five.

Then I went to the parallel bars (which are bars for gymnastics), started doing flips. Dev gave up begging me to play. He started another game.

I watched.

Fortnite was interesting.

I didn't understand why it was so popular. I mean, it looked fun. I just didn't really understand video games. Basically, one hundred players got dropped off onto an island and had to fight to the death. It was like *Hunger Games*. The last man standing (or team) won.

I didn't have time for video games, unfortunately.

I was learning Spanish, breakdancing, skating, swimming, and a few other things. Plus, school. Plus, Julie. The girl I liked. She took up a lot of my time. I wasted a little too much time thinking about her. Sometimes I got lost in daydreams about her when I was supposed to be working.

Plus, there was that.

I wasn't rich like Dev, so I had to work.

I worked at Hollister.

Anyway, I know what you're all waiting for. You probably read the back of this book and realized that I had an experience similar to *Fortnite* but in real life. It's true. And it happens soon.

Keep reading, because life as you know it is about to turn upside-down.

Ready?

You only think you are.

5

GAME DAY.

Game day was an exciting day for everyone in high school. Maybe it isn't for you. But it is for everyone in my school, because the principal had instituted a rule that if you went to game night to support your football team, you got free gift bags.

They were mystery gift bags.

We never knew what we were going to get.

One night, every student got an Xbox.

One night, every student got a shiny penny.

One night, every student got one hundred dollars cash.

Also, the principal made game night super fun.

There was much more to do than just watch the game.

There was loads of free popcorn (our principal didn't believe in health-food initiatives because the kids never ate the food; he did believe in exercise, though, which is why every week we had extra PE days but they were comprised of laser tag, jump roping, dancing competitions, martial arts, bean bag races, mega-trampoline competitions, and a bunch of other fun stuff; and there were always really cool prizes for winning), coffee on tap, cotton candy, mazes, games, arcade systems, *Fortnite* tournaments on giant screens, and much more.

Our principal didn't believe at all in something he referred to as "relativism." He believed in truth. And he believed that when you won at something it was because you were talented, had the most practice, or were the best. Therefore, in our school, there are winners and losers. When you come in first place in a game, you win something awesome. Sometimes cash. Sometimes extra credit points. When you lose, you get nothing. Not even a participation ribbon.

Since it was game night, we were all planning on being there.

Even Dev, who was usually a shut-in.

He was looking forward to beating everyone in the school at *Fortnite*—at least that's what he said he was going to do. I told him I'd watch.

I was looking forward to the breakdance competition and the hoops challenge. The hoops challenge was a game the students played against the faculty (AKA, the robots). The problem is, they had the "hoops challenge" every game night and not one student, not even our best basketball players, were able to beat the school faculty—

which was more proof that they were robots.

Anyway, I was going to try to beat them tonight.

Because why not?

Right now, I was sitting in math class. It was cool. Our math teacher taught math by doing calculations from *Star Wars* movies. Our math classroom was decked out with all kinds of *Star Wars* decorations. The entire ceiling was a giant TV screen that made it look like we were in a spaceship and we were moving through space. It was pretty cool.

And the teacher was super fun.

Which is another reason we suspected he was a robot.

Every time one of us got an answer right, he would do a backflip.

He was doing a lot of backflips right now, landing them all perfectly.

Then the bell rang.

Our bell didn't make the sound of a typical school bell. It actually played eighties music, which we all appreciated. Today it was playing *Duran Duran*.

I strapped on my skates and rode out of that class, into the wide hall.

Unlike your school hallways, our hallways smelled great. Apparently, Petrov had great-smelling stuff pumped through the air-conditioning systems. That, and we had a fleet of janitors that kept everything sparkling shiny. The floors were always in perfect condition, not one spot or speck or piece of trash. We suspected, for obvious reasons, that the janitors were also NPC bots.

Skating down the hall, I stayed on the right side.

I started going fast.

I had a twenty minute break.

There were no speed rules in our school.

You could travel however fast you wanted.

We were all required to be professional skaters.

The hallway had flashing DJ-type lights along the walls. Glowing planets hung down from the ceiling creating a cool ambience, as if we were actually in a roller-skating rink in outer space.

Eighties music was playing throughout the halls.

And I was going fast.

My plan was to travel down this hall, exit into the amphitheater, do some tricks with my friends on the stairs, grind a few rails, grab a snack from the shack, cool down, go to my next class.

That was all ruined when Gavin showed up out of nowhere.

He was riding towards me from the side, FAST.

And this wouldn't be the first time.

He regularly tried to check me into walls. If you're unfamiliar with the word "check", it's a hockey term that means to ram someone into the nearest wall. He was coming at me, perfectly angled, and only a few seconds away. If I didn't do something he would ram me into the wall on my right. Like I said, it's happened to me before. And it's no fun.

To make matters worse, right then I noticed Julie out of the corner of my eye. She was stepping out of her locker (did I mention we have walk-in lockers the size of closets?). I saw the blue in her hair (she'd died her hair a light shade of blue that she'd purchased from Hayley Williams' company).

I was about to get tackled into the wall by the school bully in front of the girl I liked.

What was I supposed to do?!

6

With the few seconds I had to react, I ducked, making myself small, continuing skating super fast. Gavin, my main enemy, coming in fast, hit me full on!

He tripped over the top of me and his body slammed into the wall.

I was sprawled out on the floor, unsure of what had happened except that I probably looked like an idiot in front of Julie. I got to my feet (skates) as fast as I could, but now Gavin was on his feet (skates), taking steps towards me. I tried to skate backwards but he got a hold of my shirt and put me in a headlock.

"My name is Allen Diaz and I'm a noob," Gavin said.

"Say it!"

"No," I said, struggling against him.

"Say it, Allen. My name is Allen Diaz, and I'm a noob."

"Let him go," I heard Julie yelling, skating towards us.

I didn't need Julie's help. She was cool to help, but it was kind of annoying to get a girl's help. I was trying to get out of the headlock when one of the hall monitors (robots), skated towards us and said, "Release Allen Diaz."

Gavin let go, raising his hands. "We were only messing around," he protested.

"Allen," asked the robot (though we were obviously supposed to think the guy was a real human), "is this true? Were you guys only 'messing around?'"

I nodded, straightening out my shirt, aware that Julie was right there watching the situation, seeing my red face from being in the headlock.

The hall monitor scanned us with a medical device to make sure we had no injuries. "All right then, continue your play. But be careful. And always believe in yourself."

Then the robot skated away.

"That was messed up, Gavin," said Julie. To me, she said, "Are you okay, Allen?"

It was nice to see her, and it was nice of her to ask me that, but I was kind of angry.

"You don't have to help me," I said. "I'm fine on my own."

"Wow," she said, crossing her arms. "I just thought we were friends and friends are supposed—"

"We are, but—"

"C'mon, Julie," said Gavin, interrupting. "We have

class and then practice afterwards."

Julie glared at me, then turned around and walked with Gavin.

Gavin was my one and only bully. I was popular at school, with all the groups, even the football players (except for Gavin). So it was weird that I had a bully. He was the only one, and it bugged the heck out of me. I know martial arts and I could easily kick his butt, but I didn't want to hurt him too badly. I could have gotten out of the headlock but I would have had to hurt him really bad and I didn't want to. But if he kept picking on me more, I would have to.

It would suck for him, but I would have no choice.

I hoped Julie would understand.

Because she was friends with Gavin.

They even dated a little sometimes. I still hadn't asked out Julie, but I knew I would be better for her than Gavin. Gavin was just a dumb jock who bullied people smaller than him.

Again, I didn't understand why he picked on me. I was shorter than him; I'm actually pretty short—but I'm not small. I have muscles, workout all the time. Heck, I have six pack abs.

Whatever.

I'd deal with it another day.

Tonight was game night, and I had to go over my breakdance routine for the competition. I put a smile on my face, played off the incident, and skated down the hall. I ran into a bunch of friends along the way, fist-bumping, hand-shaking, shouting to one another.

Then I was outside, skating through the open courtyard.

I jumped over a trash can and rolled fast down a hill towards some ramps.

I jumped onto the half-pipe and did a small routine. My friends were cheering me on. "Dancing Diaz! Get it! Get it!"

I tore it up, getting over all my angry feelings towards Gavin. Then I found my breakdancing friends and we got to work.

If I won the competition tonight, I would win a Camaro.

A freakin' Camaro!

Brand new, yellow and striped like the one in the first *Transformers* movie.

I needed a car, for sure.

Gavin had an old-fashioned Mustang, and Julie valued guys with nice cars because her dad was a mechanic. My plan was to win the competition, get the car, then get the girl.

I hadn't had a girlfriend yet since coming into high school.

Julie was the only girl I truly had a crush on.

My plan was to win the car, and I think I would have, except that everything got terribly ruined in the blink of an eye. And when I say everything, I mean EVERYTHING.

Basically I had three things planned for the night. Thinking about them made me lightheaded and nervous. Step one: win the breakdancing competition. Step two: Get the car. Step three: ask Julie out. Sure, we'd had a fight earlier in the hall, but isn't that how all great couples start off—with a fight? At least that's how they start in the movies.

I wasn't nervous about the first two steps.

The third one made me dizzy.

I decided not to think about it.

"You got this. You're the best breakdancer I've seen among people our age. I've seen some better ones on

Youtube, but you're for sure the best in real life that I know."

Dev was giving me a pep talk.

We were in his room.

I was sitting on his dirt bike, revving it up. I did some quick donuts, tearing up his floor. He didn't care. He was going to get rid of the current flooring and replace it in a week, so he wanted to tear it all up and destroy it. We threw paint all over it, spilled our grape juice. We were full on messing around. We never go half send. Only full send, all the time.

I crashed the dirt bike into the floor, letting it slide across a greased up hardwood section. Then I went to the gymnastics equipment and started doing flips as he pumped eighties dubstep remixes. Like, eighties songs remixed with dubstep.

Finally, we got dressed.

I spent thirty minutes doing my hair, getting the gel just right. Then I put on a suit that I kept in Dev's closet.

"Looking fly, Diaz," Dev said.

I entered his walk-in closet, which was bigger than my room.

I was looking fly.

"Dancin' D about to get the dub."

"When you try to talk cool, it just sounds weird," I said.

"True," said Dev. "But that is nerd lingo. It's *Fortnite* lingo."

"I know. Still."

I straightened my bow-tie.

We had one of Dev's limos take us to game night. Dev

dressed up in a fully white suit—white pants, shirt, coat, tie and everything. He was looking fleek on his way to the *Fortnite* tournament. We both had a lot to win. And a lot to lose. Especially me.

The thought of Julie with her cute blonde-hair-died blue was in my head, and I couldn't shake it. I tried, tried thinking of other things. I would focus up when the competition started.

We pulled up to the school lot and climbed out of the limo.

We walked just like we'd planned, side-by-side, looking fly.

I'd taught Dev how to walk cool. Before I'd taught him, he'd walked like a strange nerd and didn't stand up straight. We looked cool together. I put on my sunglasses even though the sun was setting.

I saw Gavin arriving in his Mustang with Julie in the passenger seat.

It made my heart ache, but I decided that all the more I would ask her out tonight. If she didn't know how I felt about her, then how could I blame her for not liking me? I needed to tell her, whether or not she rejected me.

But I hoped against all hope that she wouldn't reject me.

The school was decked out. Spotlights were shooting up into the sky. There were several clubs in several of the buildings. There was an eighties club, a nineties club, a space club, a nerd club (they played no music and solved math equations), a goth club (they played dark music and had a selection of eyeliner that any goth would be jealous of), a video game club (which was a giant auditorium decked out with thousands of TVs hooked up with different game systems and games—tonight, there was a big *Counter Strike* tournament as well as the *Fortnite* one). There were more clubs I didn't even know about.

Confetti shot up into the air everywhere.

There were fire pits and bands and clowns and even a small circus attraction. There was a petting zoo with elephants (everyone loves elephants), and a movie theater that was playing repeated viewings of *The Lion King*. Still, you only got the gift bags if you attended at least an hour of the football game.

I waved to Julie. She'd seen me getting out of the limo. She smiled and waved back. That was a good sign. I continued walking, then almost tripped over a curb. To save myself I did a side flip. It looked like I'd done it on purpose and a small group of students who'd been arriving cheered. I looked to Julie; she was smiling big. I gave a small bow, then continued onward, through the front gates of the school where two robots greeted me with cake pops.

I accepted them gratefully.

Ate one with one bite.

Tossed the other into a trash can.

I needed to eat healthy for my abs.

Then I was at the breakdancing competition.

Getting warmed up.

Tonight was the night.

I could feel it.

It was about an hour later, when the competition started, that everything went wrong. I'll tell you in the next chapter. After that chapter, the craziest thing happens. Many of you probably ride school busses. But has your school bus ever turned into a battle bus and taken off into the sky? No, well that's basically what happened to us... *Sort of.* In a way. You'll see.

Who's "us?"

Keep reading to find out.

8

ALLEN DIAZ.

My name flashed up on the large screen above the dance floor. The dance floor was lit. Literally. It was flashing all different colors, and the colors were racing around the floor, purples, pinks, blues, reds. They were synced to the loud music. Subwoofers hung all around the ceiling. Our principal, the billionaire, Nicolas Petrov, believed in bass tones. In loud music. In having lots of fun. In enjoying our youth while we had it. He gave a speech once a year and brought all three schools together. His speech was always the same. "Youth is precious. You only have it for so long. Enjoy it. Don't mess it up." He liked us to have fun. But he also wanted us to learn and do awesome things. "When you get old, you can't do sports as well anymore," he'd said. "It's harder to learn new skills when you're old. Learn while you're young. Don't waste your life or your time. Work hard. Make something of your life. You're all special. You all have meaning. God loves you all and wants you to live a great life that blesses yourself and others. So live. Truly live. And live full."

His words stuck with me.

I'd recorded them on a video on my phone and I watched them every once in awhile for inspiration anytime I got down in my emotions. When he spoke, I felt like he was speaking to me.

I'd had my headphones in and was playing that portion of the video.

I took them out.

It was my turn to dance.

I walked out on the dance floor and the DJs cued up my song. I'd worked out this routine for months. It included all my best breakdancing moves, including the air flare, the flare, and the windmill, including a bunch of other stuff and a bunch of gymnastics flips.

I was the last one to dance.

Everyone had already gone before me.

Outside the tournament room, I could hear cheers from the crowds at the football stadium. The game would start in five minutes.

All of my fear and anxiety went away as I walked onto the dance floor. I took a breath and I was focused. I knew I was going to nail the routine. Sometimes you can just tell.

My song started playing.

I started breaking. (Which is a term in breakdancing that means I started *dancing*).

I was owning. I felt in full control of my body. I was doing six-step to flare, then I jumped in mid-air to an air flare. The next step was to jump out of that to a spinning handstand.

I launched into a one-handed handstand.

I held myself on the one hand, spinning in a circle.

That's when a heavy football hit my arm and caused me to collapse on the ground. I twisted my arm back in a weird way and pain flashed up the entire right side of my body.

I collapsed onto the ground.

Looking up, wanting to scream in pain but holding it in, I saw Gavin running out of the room, and I knew it had been him. He'd chucked that football at me and ruined my whole routine.

I leapt to my feet and tried to continue, but my arm was in so much pain.

Instead, I started doing flips—side flips and backflips and other things to try to save my dance. But I knew the truth even as I tried to make up for the football interference: I was going to lose.

And even if they gave me a retry I wouldn't be able to do the routine.

I knew what was wrong with my arm. My shoulder had gotten popped out of its socket. I would need someone to pop it back in and then I would need to rest for at least a day or two so that I wouldn't hurt myself worse.

It was over.

I wasn't going to get the car.

Or the girl.

My song ended.

I walked to my nearest friend. He looked sad for me.

"That's a rough beat," he said.

"Pop my shoulder back in," I said, turning around so that he could do what he had to do. We were friends through gymnastics so I knew he knew how to relocate shoulders.

He grabbed my arm and got me into position.

"It was Gavin, wasn't it?" I asked.

"Yeah," he said.

Then he popped my shoulder back in.

I roared in pain, sweat dripping off my hair, down my forehead.

A robot faculty member came by and scanned me for injuries. Said I was fine but I would need to ice my shoulder. Then he skated away.

I was beyond angry, and I knew what I had to do.

I could hear the crowd counting down from sixty.

The football game was going to start in sixty seconds.

I was going to ruin the game for Gavin.

That's what I was going to do.

9

There was at least one thousand people in the stands. Maybe more. They were stomping on the bleachers, doing the wave, throwing around popcorn and cotton candy, hyped for the game. We had one of the best football teams. I didn't notice them.

I was focused and angry and letting it get the better of me.

I'd never been this angry in my life.

I couldn't believe Gavin had done that.

I was full-on sprinting through the school, towards the football field.

Around the field was a waist-high chain-link tall fence.

I would be able to jump it easily.

I could hear everyone counting down.

10.

9.

8.

I didn't care what happened to me. Gavin ruined something for me and hurt me. I didn't care that he was the school's star quarterback. I didn't care if I got expelled. I didn't even care what Julie would think of me.

7.

I didn't slow down.

In fact, I sped up.

6.

5.

4.

I was almost to the field.

Almost to the fence.

3.

2.

A song was playing over the loud speakers.

I hopped the fence into the field.

1.

The ball was snapped back to Gavin.

The game had officially started.

I was running across the field, directly towards Gavin.

He didn't see me yet. The team wasn't really noticing. The people on the sidelines were noticing, though. And the crowd. I could hear them reacting to me.

Then I was there.

I tackled Gavin from the side. Even though he was bigger than me, I'd been running fast and I plowed him into the soft grass. Then I ripped off his helmet and started wailing on him, pounding him in the face. Suddenly other football players were coming at me to tackle me off of him. I side-kicked one and sent him flying. I double punched another, knocking him down. I back tripped another. I did a side flip over one, then jumped back towards Gavin who was trying to get up. I could see referees (who I also suspected were robots) running towards me.

But before they could reach us, Julie was right there. She was a cheerleader, so she'd run over from the sideline.

"Stop!" she yelled, raising a hand to my face and to Gavin's. Gavin had gotten up and was trying to come at me. "Stop it you two! I've had enough of both of you!"

Gavin tried to move past her. She blocked him with her small body as if she were some kind of giant. I was breathing heavy, still angry. I wasn't sure what to do.

Part of me couldn't believe what I'd just done.

But Gavin had deserved it.

Right?

Everything started to feel like a dream. The crazy noise of the wild crowd, the referees yelling, all the other teammates yelling at me, was all muted background noise. I didn't even notice it. As far as I could tell, the only people that currently existed was Julie, Gavin, and I.

"You don't know what he did!" I yelled to Julie, trying to justify my actions.

"I'm sure he did something terrible, but I expected more from you, Allen."

That cut me in my heart, and suddenly my anger subsided.

Apparently Gavin's anger didn't. He pushed past her and punched me in the face. My world faded to black. I'd been knocked unconscious.

And when I woke up, nothing in my life was ever the same again.

10

I woke up in the nurses' office.

I was laying on those uncomfortable beds with the thin paper on top of it. There was an IV in my hand. It was weird. Everything in our school was ultra-modern and ultra-high-tech, except for the nurses' offices. Those were old-fashioned looking.

There was a pretty nurse at the other end of the room, in an office chair, holding an iPad.

I lifted my hand, indicating the IV. "Was it really that bad?"

She looked up from her iPad. Looked back down at it and pressed a few buttons. Then looked up from it. She smiled.

But then I fell back asleep.

I woke up again, in the same spot.

But this time no nurse was here. The IV was still connected to the back of my hand. I watched a liquid that looked like water seep into it. Except the liquid wasn't exactly clear.

It turned blue as it went into my hand.

My heart beat a little.

I looked around the small room. I hoped the liquid was okay. It looked weird, like *Windex*. I watched it travel into my hand. It gave my hand a funny tingling sensation.

I sat up on the uncomfortable bed.

I watched the closed door.

All of the sudden, the door burst open and a man I instantly recognized but was shocked to see stepped through. Nicolas Petrov: our billionaire principal who hardly ever showed up but once a year for his speech. I'd never talked to him in person. I'd never even been this close to him.

I was shocked, and my mouth was hanging open.

"You'll be fine, son," he said.

"What are—how are—" I didn't know what to say.

"Take the IV out of your hand," he said.

"What—who—me?!"

Was he really asking me to take a giant needle out of my hand?

He stepped up to me. "Should I do it?"

"I guess—"

"They're putting *Windex* in you," he said.

I looked up at him to see if he was joking. His face was

solid. Didn't look like he was joking at all. Then I saw a slight smile cross his face and I breathed easier.

"Wait," I finally said. "Shouldn't you wait for the nurse?"

He pulled the tape off my hand. Then he yanked the needle out of my hand.

"Owww," I grunted.

"You're in big trouble, kid," he said.

"So you ripped the IV out of my hand?"

"No. You're punishment is not that, though that was fun. You made a noise like a little girl."

"Did not."

"Either way, you've got detention. Big time."

"What are you doing here, sir?" I said. "Surely my ruining the game couldn't have been that big of a deal for you to have come all the way out here."

"I come when I must," he said. "And I must."

"Why?"

"Surely you must know, Allen Diaz."

"Know what?"

"Follow me."

He led the way out of the nurses' offices, down a few hallways then to a giant door that had a padlock on it. He unlocked it. We stepped through into an antechamber that had a giant vault. He opened it using a giant combination lock. Through this door was a giant room that looked like an aquarium. As we stepped through, I saw that it was an aquarium.

We went down an escalator, and over our heads and all around was a giant tank of water with swimming fish and sharks and all kinds of stuff.

"This is under the school!" I said, shocked.

Petrov said nothing.

"How come no one knows about this?"

"I know about it," he said.

"Does anyone else?" I said. "Because I've never heard about it at all. From anyone."

"Only a few people."

"Which few?" I asked.

"You'll see."

The escalator went down and down and down. I wondered how far underground we were. Until finally the escalator stopped beside a walkway that led us to seats in a tubular thing that looked like a roller coaster. "Get in," he said.

I climbed into one of the seats on the long roller coaster.

He sat beside me.

The track extended out ahead of us into darkness. I couldn't see where it went.

"This is some kind of roller coaster?" I said.

"Strap in," he said.

He lowered the seatbelt over himself.

I did the same.

"Prepare for the ride of your life," an overhead speaker said.

"Three," the speaker said. "Two. One."

The sound of rockets going off reached my ears.

BLAST!

The coaster took off, like crazy, like nothing I'd experienced and I'd been on all the roller coasters at Disneyland, Disney World, and Knott's Berry Farm. The thing flew in the darkness. Air was rushing past us. I couldn't see anything. Couldn't hear anything except for my own screaming. I remembered Petrov had made fun of me for saying "ouch," when he'd pulled out the IV, so I stopped screaming. Looking around, I strained to see anything.

Suddenly a light far away that looked like a star flashed to life, accompanied by the noise of a single synth note—as if someone had concurrently pressed a key on a synth. Another star lit up, accompanied by another noise. This continued happening.

Suddenly the sky was filled with stars.

"Where are we?" I yelled, figuring Petrov wasn't going to answer.

He didn't.

Then we were flying upwards, towards the stars.

More and more stars were appearing and it seemed like we would hit one of them. Our coaster started dodging them, going different directions—fast turns to the right and left. We even went upside-down a few times.

THEN, finally, the roller coaster stopped.

All the stars turned off.

Once again, we were in total and replete darkness.

Until a giant overhead spotlight turned on. I could see a platform beside us. Our seatbelts released. I climbed out. Petrov followed.

Then he past me up.

"This way," he said in his Russian accent.

As he walked down the platform into areas of darkness, more overhead spotlights flashed on, illuminating our way. I could see now that we were on a platform about four feet wide. On either side the platform dropped off into darkness. Far below us I could see water, hundreds of feet below.

Suddenly I was afraid.

I have great balance, and four feet is a lot, but I was just so confused.

"Where the heck are we?" I asked.

"Almost there," he said. "Keep up. We have much to do."

11

Finally, at the end of the long platform was a door marked with a placard that read: DETENTION. It was a basic door, like the kinds of doors that led into our classrooms. Petrov pushed through the door and what I saw shocked me.

It was like a small movie theater, with movie theater seats that were slanted downwards toward a screen. I saw the back of a few people's heads.

They turned around to look at us.

Their mouths dropped open upon seeing Petrov.

"Allen," said Julie, shocked to see both of us walking in together.

What were they doing here?

There were three students here: my best friend Dev, my worst enemy Gavin, and my greatest crush Julie. Just us. And Petrov.

"Have a seat," Petrov instructed me.

"What are you guys—" I started to ask, but Petrov cut me off by saying, "No talking!"

I stopped, took a seat next to all of them.

We were sitting in one row.

I looked back to Petrov, but he was gone.

Suddenly, music, like, orchestra music, started playing. Really beautiful music that you hear in cool movies like *The Last Samurai*, or *Open Range*, or *Lord of the Rings*. But the screen stayed black. Finally an image faded from black onto the screen.

It was a picture of the four of us—Gavin, Dev, Julie, and I.

Someone had done a painting of us, looking super cool, standing back to back, like some sort of squad or something. We were wearing bright and colorful outfits, as if we were characters in a video game, and we were holding various weapons that looked like video game type of weapons.

Then a video of Petrov himself showed up on the screen.

"You four were hand selected for the greatest adventure of your lives. Welcome to detention." I just realized it was freezing cold in this movie-theater room. I was only wearing a t-shirt. I hugged myself, goosebumps forming.

Suddenly the seats beneath us were rumbling.

"Put on your glasses," Petrov instructed.

Glasses fell into our laps from apparently the ceiling.

3D glasses.

I put mine on.

Suddenly the image of Petrov was just in front of me, and it seemed like he was looking into my eyes. "You all did something very bad today. But, you are all chosen, nonetheless."

I wondered what Dev and Julie had done to deserve detention.

I knew Gavin and I deserved it, but...

Then the clips of each of our wrongdoings started playing on the screen. Gavin chucking that football at me in the middle of my dance routine. Me tackling Gavin. Apparently Dev had seen what was happening—had seen me running towards the field—he'd joined the fight after and had tried to kick Gavin but he'd ended up getting tackled by someone. And then one of the cheerleader girls started yelling at Julie for standing up to Gavin and Allen. The girl pulled Julie's hair and Julie punched her in the face, knocking her out.

Jeez, I thought.

I'd started a big fight.

I wondered why the cheerleader girl who had fought with Julie wasn't here. Neither was the football player who had tackled Dev.

"Why us?" I asked the video even though I realized it was just a video.

"Because, Allen," said the video of Petrov, "you four are special."

"Except for Gavin," said Dev.

Gavin got out of his seat to punch Dev, but a seat belt strap type of thing shot out, wrapped around Gavin, pulled him back into his chair. He got sucked back into the chair with a GRUNT.

Then the image of Petrov disappeared.

A video of another guy, who was wearing a uniform and looked like a military captain popped up on the screen.

"You're about to be dropped into another world," the man said. He was standing in what looked like a plane hangar. "Everything you thought you knew is going to be turned upside-down. This is a good thing. Don't fret. Only fight. You four, though you have your differences, are a team, and your objective is a simple one. You're going to have to save the world."

I got shivers down my spine.

Something was happening. Something big.

I didn't quite know what.

But I knew it was going to be amazing.

12

"You're going to have to work together," the man on the screen said. "Nicolas Petrov will be your leader."

We all looked at each other.

"There are necklaces under each of your seats. Reach for them now and put them on."

I reached under and found mine. It was a small circular pendant. On it was etched in the word: WORTHY. I looked to the others, couldn't see their words.

I draped it over my neck.

The moment it fell over my neck it started glowing BLUE.

I held it up, saw that it still said the word, WORTHY,

except now the word was glowing. The others' necklaces were glowing blue as well.

"To Gavin, HUMILITY," the man on the screen said. "To Dev, COURAGE." I looked over and saw them fingering the pendants on their necklaces. "To Julie, STRENGTH." "And to Allen, WORTHINESS." The man on the video smiled at us, held the smile for a few seconds. "These are yours to keep. Keep them around your necks at all times and don't lose them or something very bad will happen. Don't lose them because they are the key to everything. They unlock what you need to win."

I was so lost, but still in awe.

What was about to happen?

What was happening?

Then the man in the video climbed into an airplane, the old-fashioned kind that flew in the first World Wars. He took off into the skies and we watched him fly over a beautiful looking island. He was wearing a headset and he talked into it. His voice sounded like it was coming through a radio now.

"Beautiful, isn't it?" he said. "It's called Death Island, and it's where you're going. A Battle Royale scenario. You'll be dropped on the island as a team, to face many other teams in the amount of two hundred. Two hundred teams. Eight hundred players total. Winning the game is simple. Be the last team alive."

"What happens if we die?" Dev asked.

The man couldn't hear us.

The video was probably pre-recorded.

"After you land on the island," he said, "be sure to collect as much equipment and supplies as possible. You'll need it. You'll need weapons too. Think fast, follow your instincts, and you might make it. After all, you were chosen for a reason."

Then the man jumped out of the plane.

We watched him soar down in a downwards dive until finally, when he was dangerously close to the land, he pulled out his parachute.

He landed on the top of a giant mountain. The view around him was beautiful. The mountain was covered in beautiful trees and overlooked a valley of different types of ecosystems and settings. "Don't let the island's beauty fool you. It's replete with tricksters, gangs, monsters, and hotheads. A spell has been cast over the island. A spell not easily broken. You see, sea creatures from the surrounding ocean have been altered, through an evil scientist's 'spell'"—the word 'spell' he put into quotations with his fingers—"and the creatures are invading the land, pressing in from all sides. Don't get caught near the creatures. You can't kill them. They will kill you. Because of the sea creatures, you and the other teams will be forced to the center of the island, which will force you to have to face and fight each other.

"Death Island is not for cowards. It's for the daring. It's not for losers. It's for the bold. Stay close together. Don't split up. You'll have better chances as a team."

The man tapped his ear. "You'll be given ear chips. You'll be able to hear each other and talk to each other if and in fact you get split up, but only to a certain distance. If you're a few hundred meters apart you'll lose contact. I repeat, stay close together.

"May God be with you, students. Fight hard. Never surrender. Never give up."

Then the screen turned to black.

We waited there in the theater in stunned silence.

Finally I looked to my right at Dev. Then to my left at Julie.

A video of Petrov came on the screen. "While you were watching," he said, "I primed our plane. Exit to the door marked with the EXIT SIGN. Watch your step, players. And prepare your minds. Death Island is kind to no one."

The video cut off.

The house lights turned on.

A door at the bottom of the steps on the left opened and light flooded inward.

We all stood at the same time.

Walked down the stairs.

Through the door.

And that's when everything started.

Welcome To Death Island

1

Right outside the movie theater room was the SCHOOL BUS.

It was blue.

Kind of like the Battle Bus in *Fortnite*, except that it actually wasn't a school bus. It was one of those old-fashioned World War II types of airplanes. Painted on the side was the word "School Bus" as well as assorted phrases, logos and symbols.

I recognized some of the logos—large gaming and energy drink companies. That was interesting. Petrov was wearing an expensive-looking three-piece suit, as if he'd just come from one of his billionaire business meetings.

"Empty your pockets," he said, and held a bucket before us. "Everything."

I emptied my wallet, which had a few dollars and my school ID. I also emptied my chapstick and a napkin and my cell phone. We emptied everything into the buckets.

"Climb in," he said, indicating the old airplane.

"What if we don't want to?" asked Julie.

Which was a good question to ask.

Because this whole thing was crazy.

But it was the kind of crazy that I liked. I had thought to ask the question, but I hadn't asked because I wanted to go to Death Island. I wanted to fight on a squad.

"You have no choice," Petrov said flatly. "You're in detention."

We climbed into the spacious propeller plane. Petrov came in after us and slid into the main pilot's chair. "I will need a co-pilot," he said.

Then he handed back a tray of four ear chips.

I remembered them from the orientation video, put one in my ear.

When Petrov said his next sentence I could hear him perfectly in my left ear. "Dev, you will be my co-pilot. You're good at video games."

Dev gladly accepted this roll.

Petrov pressed a button, and the large bay door we'd just entered shut behind us.

The cabin was dark, until it powered on. Dim lights turned on around the ceiling. The propellers began firing, twisting with a fury like I'd never before seen.

Next thing I knew we were driving down the street, down an alley, into one of the school parking lots that I recognized. Then we were on a street I recognized. Cars were all around us, passing us, honking at us. Then some police cars showed up behind us, sirens blaring, obviously mad that our giant plane was on normal neighborhood roads.

"What should we do?" Dev asked Petrov.

Petrov shrugged. "They can't catch us."

Then we entered a freeway onramp.

Once up the ramp, Petrov yelled: "MAX POWER!"

Dev did something, and we started rolling super fast down the freeway, passing cars on each side. It felt kind of like this one time I went to camp—climbing in a bus and taking off on an adventure with my friends. Except we were in a freakin' airplane, on a freeway, and cars and police were mad all around us.

Finally, Petrov lifted up on the steering wheel and the giant old hunk of metal lifted into the sky. Headed right towards a bridge that extended over the freeway!

2

"Bridge!" Gavin shouted, holding onto a handrail along the ceiling of the airplane. I gripped the handrail opposite his. Julie was holding Gavin's arm, which was making me a little jealous. They weren't even an official thing. They'd only dated a little. Why wasn't she holding my arm? Guess she was still mad at me. But, still, what Gavin had done was way worse.

Why not me?

Annoyed, I peered through the front window and saw that Gavin's concern was well directed. We were headed directly towards that bridge.

"Up, up, up," Julie was saying.

Dev seemed calm in the co-pilot's seat, though, and I trusted him. Knew he had flying skills from all the simulation games he played in his room. He had full virtual reality setups.

We sliced over the top of the bridge, just making it over the top of a tall semi-truck.

Then we were flying straight towards the thin and sporadic clouds in the sky.

Airborne.

I couldn't believe any of this stuff was happening.

I just then started thinking of my parents. My dad would be pretty angry at me if he found out what I was up to. Death Island and the whole thing sounded fun in one sense and terrible in another. What if we died? What if *Julie* died?

I glanced over at her as the plane rumbled all around us.

She was so pretty, I lost my breath.

She must have noticed me looking at her because she looked over.

We made eye contact, but then she looked away from me.

Still angry.

Now I was annoyed again. I wanted to say, "What's your problem? Gavin ruined my chances at winning a car. I have no money! I needed that car. All I have is breakdancing and my skills. Gavin already has a car and rich parents and he's the immensely popular star quarterback."

But I knew it best not to bring all that up right now.

We were climbing high and fast, coming up over the mountains that edged in the valley in which we lived.

Straight towards the clouds. Petrov and Dev were talking to each other, saying complicated pilot stuff I didn't understand.

Finally, after bursting very high very fast, the plane leveled out. It stopped rumbling so much and the hum all around us softened. I released the hand rail, looking around the plane. I saw a mini-fridge in the back corner, next to some cabinets. Other than the fridge, there was nothing else.

Opening it, there were some water bottles and energy drinks.

I took a water bottle. Chugged half of it.

Then popped open a can of one of my favorite kinds of energy drinks. Sipped it. It tasted great. I grabbed another one to bring to Dev.

Gavin was at the fridge now, pushing me aside.

I pushed back. He went to attack me.

Julie stepped between us.

"Guys!" she yelled.

That calmed Gavin down.

I continued walking towards the cockpit. Brought Dev the drink. When I went to hand it to him, Petrov grabbed it. "Thank you," he said.

"Actually that was for..."

But Petrov had already popped it and was drinking it.

"Excuse me, sir," I said, "but I don't understand any of this. How is this even happening? How are you not going to get in big trouble for taking off in a plane on the freeway? That's got to be against a hundred laws."

"I'm a billionaire. I can get away with almost anything."

"Is Death Island like laser tag or is it real? I mean, are

we really at risk of death?"

"Wait and see," he said. "No more questions. Let Dev and I fly."

I went back to the fridge, didn't see Julie or Gavin in this area of the plane. There was a closed door. They must have gone through it. I brought Dev an energy drink, then went back to the closed door. Going through it, I saw there was a small room of bunk beds. Gavin and Julie were seated on one of the tall ones, talking and drinking their energy drinks.

I took the top bunk across from them.

Suddenly feeling very tired.

Yawning, I said, "Are you guys tired?"

They were yawning, which answered my question.

I took another big gulp of my energy drink.

"Maybe these aren't energy drinks," I said, looking at the label. Upon closer inspection, I saw that *they actually weren't the drinks I thought they were.* They were made to look like energy drinks, but they were "sleeping" drinks, packed with enough sleeping ingredients to knock out a horse.

We were all yawning a lot.

I was leaned against the back wall, looking at Julie and Gavin together.

Oftentimes, when humans are sleepy, we have a tendency to say things we wouldn't otherwise say, SAY, first thing in the morning.

"Why?" I asked, looking directly at Julie, as Gavin rested his head on her shoulder. "Why Gavin?"

"Because," she said.

But then her eyes closed.

And then my eyes closed.

And we were all asleep.

I had a dream of when I was young and my dad and I were still best friends. But then it turned into the nightmare that is my life, of my dad threatening to punch me, of having to run away at night to Dev's house. Why didn't my dad love me? Why did he treat me so badly? The nightmare criss-crossed with Julie and Gavin. In my dream, I saw them getting married, which was weird since we were only in high school. But, still, it was my nightmare. I wondered why she liked him and not me. I knew I had a lot of friends and was very popular, but why did the people who mattered to me the most not like me?

I woke up instantaneously, snapping out of my crazy dreams. Bullets were flying through our plane, punching through the metal and ricocheting around the interior.

I jumped out of the bunk bed, covering my head.

Gavin and Julie jumped down behind me.

A few bullets punched through the metal floor under my feet. I jumped back, yelling. Once they stopped, I ran forward, through the door, into the main part of the plane.

Dev and Petrov were yelling at each other.

I could hear them in my ear chip.

I was surprised they hadn't woken me up through the

ear chip. Or perhaps the ear chip had a way of knowing when we were asleep and muted itself. I didn't know, and it didn't matter.

"We need to land," I heard Dev yelling.

"We need to keep going! We're on the outer edges of the island."

So we'd made it to the island. I wondered how long I'd been asleep. But mostly I was wondering why bullets were punching into the plane. I really, really, *really* didn't want to get shot.

More bullets pierced the side of the plane.

I dropped to the ground, not that that was the safest place—considering that just moments ago bullets were coming through the ground.

Before Dev and Petrov could fight more, the propellers stopped spinning. With a sputter, the engine stopped working. Just shut off.

"That can't be good," said Gavin.

"You think?!" said Julie.

I grabbed a hand rail, back on my feet.

Our plane started falling out of the sky.

4

"We have to jump," yelled Petrov.

Then he was running past us.

The plane was starting to nosedive down.

I waited for Dev to reach me, then I ran with him towards the back of the plane, following Petrov. There were exactly five parachutes.

I was only fourteen and I definitely had not jumped out of a plane. Though I did understand the concept. I threw on my chute, clipped it together. Then I turned my attention to Dev and Julie to make sure they were putting theirs on right. They were both capable and strapped.

Then Petrov clicked a giant button to open the bay

door.

Bullets were flying past, still hitting the plane here and there.

Since the plane was entering a nosedive, we had to grip onto stuff to climb to the top of the bay door in order to jump out. Again, I waited for Dev and Julie to reach the top.

"Go!" I yelled to each one of them.

Julie went.

Dev went next.

Then I jumped out of a plane for the first time in my life.

The next few seconds were crazy. Some of the craziest ever. The wind was rushing all around me as I fell out of the plane. Julie's body had gotten hit by a gust of wind and she got knocked at least one hundred feet to the side. Angling my body against the wind, I flew over to her. It was so freakin' cool! Gavin was falling far off, body spread out against the wind. Dev was doing fine. Petrov was in a straight-down dive like the guy from the video had demonstrated.

I wanted to try that, but I needed to be with Julie.

I flew fast towards her, passed her up.

Then I flew back towards her, grabbed her arms.

"You good?" I yelled.

"Am now!" she yelled.

I could hear her in my ear chip as well as in person.

"Everyone good?" I asked.

Everyone answered in their own ways.

Except for Petrov. Instead, he said, "Hurry up. Dive! Or you'll get shot out of the sky."

As he said it, bullets whizzed past us.

"He's right," I said to Julie. "Let's dive."

Julie was smart and capable. We both straight-down dived, side by side. Now, for the first time since jumping out of the plane, I was looking down at the terrain beneath us. At the island. Death Island.

We were far above it, and parts of it looked dark and scary, but other parts looked warm and inviting. There were parts of it that looked like city. Parts were covered in snow. Parts were covered in trees. The terrain varied dramatically. And the sea was edging it in. I could see gigantic sea creatures, even from here—what looked like whales and squids and giant sharks—all around the island, hemming it in. I remembered what the guy in the video had said: a spell over the land. Sea creatures pressing in. Don't try to fight them.

Noted.

The wind was passing us, and I felt like a bullet, rushing down towards the ground.

"Don't pull," said Petrov, referring to our parachutes.

He was well beyond us, apparently having done this before.

Directly beneath us, we were headed for a clearing amongst trees, where there was what looked to be a giant castle. As we got nearer I realized it was some kind of castle/mansion hybrid. Or perhaps castles were mansions. By "hybrid," I meant that much of it was built of stone and much of it was built of wood. Petrov was headed directly for it.

The castle was dangerously close to the ocean.

Which is probably why Petrov had wanted to fly deeper

over the island.

But we'd gotten shot down.

I saw giant waves splashing against a wall beyond the forest. The waves were almost going to flow over the wall. When it did, it would rush through the forest and over to the castle.

I guess we had no choice, though, than to go to the castle.

"Should we land on the roof?" Dev yelled. "Like *Fortnite*."

"No," said Petrov. "This is nothing like *Fortnite*. This is real. We can't break through walls. At least not with sledgehammers. That would take too long. We need to go through the front door."

"What if it's locked?" asked Gavin.

That was actually a good question.

"I have a good feeling about this castle," said Petrov.

"What the heck is going on?" yelled Julie. Except she didn't use the word "heck." She used a very bad word instead. "Petrov, you need to explain!"

"Why didn't you guys fall asleep from the sleeping drinks?" I asked.

Dev said, "Petrov told me not to drink it. He'd only pretended to drink his because I guess he wanted you guys to drink up and conk out. He doesn't like answering questions. He's not going to explain why we were chosen. Or why we're here. I think it's best just to accept that we are here."

"My thoughts exactly," said Gavin. "Let's kick some butt."

"We deserve an explanation," said Julie.

"We're not getting one," I said. "Gavin's right."

"Shut-up, Allen!" he yelled.

I laughed.

"You will need to work together," said Petrov. Then he pulled his parachute.

We were so close to the ground that I could easily smell the ocean. And I could see the sea monsters very clearly. They looked terrifying and like nothing I'd ever seen before. Long tentacles from giant squids were shooting out of the water and slapping back down into the ocean.

The water seemed to be rising even faster.

I didn't see any squads around the mansion. It seemed safe enough. Though there were trees all around, so teams could be hiding amongst the trees.

Petrov hit the ground first, landing in the front lawn of the mansion, near a giant and *ornate*—which means really, really, heck-a-nice—water fountain.

We landed thirty seconds after Petrov, all in similar areas.

I was quick to throw off my chute and step out from under it as the giant chute fell against the grass. Petrov was running towards the mansion.

Behind us, a few hundred yards, the ocean and all the sea creatures were splashing up against the wall. In the trees, I could hear the sounds of vehicles—what sounded like ATVs and dirt bikes.

And I was right.

Two ATVs, one jeep and one dirt bike emerged from the forest. A team. They'd already found vehicles. Which meant they'd probably already found—

They started shooting towards us!

The guy in the jeep had a turret.

"Run!" I yelled, though it was a pretty obvious thing to

say and we were all already running. Julie was just as fast as us, for the most part. We had at least one hundred feet to the front door of the castle.

Please, please, please be unlocked, is all I was thinking.

Bullets were tearing into the grass around us, coming dangerously close.

We ran, ran, and ran.

Glancing overhead, I saw more planes flying over the top of the island. I watched one get shot down, burst into flames—at least ours hadn't bursted into flames.

800 people were getting dropped onto the island.

200 teams.

Was there any way we could win?

Though we were being shot at and had no weapons or armor, I had this feeling in my gut that we could. I was good at everything I did. I was supremely talented and smart. I felt that I could.

But I wondered if that feeling was an illusion.

My heart started beating even faster than it already had been.

I knew I was born for this.

I knew I was born for something great.

I recalled the time when I was nine-years-old and climbed up on my roof and asked for the aliens to come and get me. They hadn't. But this was my chance.

This strange event—this Battle Royale in real life thing with our crazy billionaire principal—this could prove everything I already thought: that I mattered.

It could.

Or it couldn't.

And that's what I feared.

If we failed, we would all be dead, or maybe some of

us.

I still wasn't sure about how all that worked.

It seemed wrong for a school principal to take us somewhere where we could actually die. But Petrov was no ordinary principal.

I knew for sure that none of this was a dream, crazy as it was.

We were within ten feet of the castle, when my question about death got answered.

Bullets from the jeep's turret hit Petrov. He got hit multiple times and blood burst from his body. He was shaking and convulsing and fell to the ground.

Gavin, Dev and I were instantly at his side, grabbing his arms and dragging him the rest of the way to the mansion. Julie opened the gigantic front doors. And we pulled Petrov into the room as bullets riddled the open front door.

Before Julie and Dev pulled the doors shut, I heard a gigantic noise like I'd never heard before—like a thunder crack but louder and longer and even more terrifying. Instead of the noise being accompanied by lightning, it was accompanied by a colossal wave. I watched the wave climb much higher than the wall that had been holding back the sea.

"Tidal wave," I muttered under my breath.

And then the doors were closed.

Julie instantly dropped a latch the length of both doors across the doors, effectively locking out the other team— the team which was soon going to be drowned by the water. At the moment, we were safe in the mansion. Maybe. The tidal wave could very well burst through the doors and drown us inside.

Instead of worrying about that, I dropped to my knees at Petrov's side. He was coughing a lot and blood was dripping from him onto the floor, forming a pool.

He sat up, on his knees, looked to all of us. "I'm dying," he said.

"This is all real," said Julie, sounding like she was about to have a breakdown.

We were too intently watching him that we weren't looking around. The wave hadn't hit the doors yet.

"Battle Royale," he said. "The last team alive wins."

He pointed to my necklace, which was still glowing blue.

"You are the BLUE TEAM. Allen is your leader. Follow him. Trust him. And you'll win." He looked to the others.

My eyes went wide. I was too shocked to react. I was watching Petrov die before my eyes. This couldn't all be real. Could it?

"If you win, you win a major prize."

Then Petrov fell onto his back and blood was coming out of his mouth.

"If you lose," he said, barely breathing. "You all die."

Those were Petrov's last words.

I felt for his pulse.

There was none.

He was literally and actually dead.

All of our faces were shocked. We looked to one another. Dev puked off to one side. Julie was crying. I was the leader. But I had no idea what to do.

That's when the giant wave of water hit the doors!

5

We were all watching the doors. They croaked against the tidal wave. Water started bursting through the seams of the door—underneath it and down the center. At first, only a little, but it was obvious that more would come through and the doors would probably break apart any moment now.

"May I help you?" a voice said.

We all turned. Coming down one of the very fancy stairways was a man, dressed like a butler and holding a tray. I couldn't see what was on the tray.

There was something off about him.

That's all I knew.

I was right, too, because he randomly started rushing towards us. I could see what was on the tray now. Knives. He took a knife off the tray, threw the rest aside, and was running across the large marbled foyer of the mansion. Towards us!

I stepped out beyond Julie, to protect her.

Gavin and I were looking at each other.

If anyone was going to be able to fight this guy, it would be us.

What was weird was he didn't have a team with him. He wasn't with a squad. At least not that we could see. And it seemed like he belonged to this house.

As he got within twenty-five feet, I saw that his eyes were red.

"Bro!" Gavin yelled to the guy. "Bro! Step back."

"He's not stopping," I said to Gavin. "I got right."

"I got this," said Gavin.

"You mean you have *left?*"

"I got this *on my own.*"

That said, Gavin took off running towards the angry butler with the bright red eyes. Water was pouring past our feet now. The door was creaking louder than ever, probably about to burst.

I ran after Gavin to help him.

He reached the butler first, grabbing the man's arm and tackling him into the ground. Then Gavin started wailing him in the face. I slid past them, across the slick floor, scooped up one of the knives the butler had tossed aside.

Then I ran back to the butler, sliding across my knees towards him as he threw Gavin off of him. The man was strong. But I stabbed him through the chest before he could make another move. I watched the red drain from his eyes as he gave up his struggle against Gavin.

Blood began to drain from the man.

I was shocked at what I'd just done.

I'd just killed a man apparently.

Dev and Julie were all there now.

The large double-doors to the castle were groaning more than ever from the weight of the water against it. I could only imagine what was happening beyond the castle doors. Which is when I heard another sound like thunder cracking—another tidal wave was headed this way.

Apparently the ocean was going to flood the island.

And the sea monsters with it.

Forcing people to run to the center and fight.

"It's like an NPC," said Dev, referring to the butler. "In this game of Battle Royale, there are teams and squads, like us, and there are NPCs."

"Which are?" asked Julie.

"Like playing against the computer in a video game rather than playing against an actual person," Gavin answered. Then he looked at me. "See, I know things."

"Never said you didn't," I said. "Next time, let's work together."

"I'm not working with you," he said.

Julie ignored us. Asked Dev, "So there are going to be more killer butlers in the house?"

"Probably. Exactly. There are probably all kinds of NPCs on this island. The sea monsters for example. They are programmed. They aren't real. But they will really kill you."

"The players are real, though?" asked Julie.

"Exactly," said Dev.

That's when the giant doors broke inward with the sound of loud and uncontainable cracks. Water burst through the doors as if it were coming out of a firehose.

Without another word, we were running towards the nearest stairway. I kept the knife in my hand as I jumped onto the stairs and started running up them three at a time.

The castle was gigantic, at least a few stories high.

I got to the second level and saw two butlers walking down the hall. They saw me, shouted, "Intruder!" and started coming towards me. Towards us.

"Keep going upstairs," I told my team.

Then I ran towards the butlers.

I was the only one with a knife, unfortunately.

But then I saw Gavin running beside me, holding the knife he must have taken from the first butler. We ran towards the butlers side by side.

"I got right."

"Fine," Gavin grunted.

I glanced back and saw Dev and Julie running up the next stairway together, which was good because we needed to get higher. But bad because there might be more evil butlers up that way.

Gavin and I were sprinting down the wide carpeted hall fast.

I didn't slow when I reached the butler. I front kicked him down to the floor. Stabbed him in the chest. Gavin tackled his, then slit his throat.

We were on our feet right away.

Back at the stairway.

I looked over the banister for a moment to see that the water was filling up the foyer fast. I was trying to think of a long-term plan. I didn't see how we could survive much longer in this castle. There would be more tidal waves. And—

That's when I saw a swordfish leap out of the water, getting a few feet of air, and nosing back in. The sea monsters were entering the castle. That couldn't be good.

6

The third floor was quiet. A little too quiet. The four of us walked down the first hall. The halls up here were wide, as you'd expect. There were lots of doors on either side of the hall. Lots of rooms. Gavin opened one at random.

It was dark inside.

He stepped in and switched on the light.

The room was completely empty. Nothing in it.

Dev went across the hall, tried another door—nothing but a bed in it.

I tried one. In it was a bed and a long chest at the end of the bed. I opened it. Inside were blankets. Nothing much we could do with those.

We tried a few more rooms and found nothing.

"Could be wasting our time," Dev said.

"Never know."

I started running down the hall. Turned the corner. Went down the next hall. This hall was different. Made of brick rather than wood. There were paintings on the wall of old people I didn't know. Didn't care. That's when I heard a distinct cry for help. Literally, I heard a man's voice yelling: "HELP!" I could tell exactly where it was coming from.

I stopped running, motioned for the others to stop.

We stood abreast, listening.

"Help me! Someone help me!"

It wasn't coming from any of the rooms around us. Just for fun, I opened a door to one of the rooms. It was a utility closet. Brooms, mops, other junk like that. Dev opened a door a little ways down—a metal door. "Jackpot!" he yelled.

"Help!" I heard the man's voice yell again. Sounded like an older man, but I couldn't really tell. We all ran down to Dev's room.

The room was filled with all kinds of weapons. Swords, knives, armor—like stuff knights of old would use. But then it also had shelves lined with guns. There were suits and suits of chainmail and armor. They all looked heavy and too big for me.

There were also guns that looked futuristic, like laser guns.

It was a lot to take in.

We started choosing our weapons.

I chose a pistol, which I tucked into the back of my pants like I'd seen Tom Cruise do in a movie. Then I grabbed a rifle that had a strap and put it around my body so that it hung on my back. I grabbed some clips of ammo but I didn't know where to put them. That's when Dev arrived at my side holding a backpack open. I started dumping clips into the bag. He'd hold them for me.

For the team.

Gavin chose a long rifle and a giant shotgun and apparently a bazooka. He was big and bulky and able to carry them. Julie chose two pistols and a small submachine gun that she could carry easily enough.

"Help!" I could still hear the man yelling.

"We should help that guy," I said.

"He's probably an NPC," said Dev. "Or a team trying to trick us and kill us."

"If he's an NPC, what does that mean?"

"It means he's a side quest, since Death Island apparently works like a video game. If we help him, he might help us."

"We need all the help we can get," I said. "Let's find him."

"We don't have time," said Gavin. "And we have weapons now."

"We still don't really know what we're doing. We don't understand this place. We need more information. We need help," I said.

"Let's split up," Gavin said. "Julie and I will go our own way."

"We need to stay together, Gavin," said Julie. "Remember what Petrov said."

Gavin objected with a curse word, turning away from

us. He walked over to the far wall with all his guns. There were very thick curtains covering a window. I hadn't noticed. He moved them aside. Light spilled into the room and the view before us was beyond imaginable.

All of the land around the castle was flooded.

And was only getting worse.

The water was clear over the land, especially because it was nice and bright outside. I saw a giant whale slowly moving through the water. I spotted a giant shark swimming into the nearby trees. The water level was only going to get higher.

"Help!" the man continued to yell.

Gavin was wrong. I knew we needed to help that guy. That's what my instincts told me. "We're helping him," I said.

Then I took off down the hall.

"Dev," I called back as I went forward. "Check more rooms. Get us more equipment. I'm going to find the man."

I ran down the hall. It curved around and I found another stairway. The man's voice was getting closer. I climbed this new stairway. Entered a much tighter hall. I hadn't seen any butlers or anything like that. But, as I approached the one door at the top of this stairway, I heard gunshots sounding off down the halls from where I'd come. I trusted Gavin would protect Julie. And I hoped he would protect Dev. Dev was weaker and less talented in real life things. He was good at video games, but not so much at real target practice and things of that nature.

I tried to open this door but it was locked.

The man's voice was much louder up here, though.

Then I remembered I had guns.

I held my rifle towards the doorknob. I'd never shot a rifle like this before. I pulled the trigger and the gun sent tons of rounds into the doorknob, nearly knocking me back. I could smell smoke coming from the gun. The door opened a bit and I stopped shooting and kicked it open. This door led into a gigantic room with lots of rooms and twin stairways leading up to a fifth floor.

I saw a maid, a woman, dressed up like a maid in the dress with the white apron, coming down one of the stairways. "How may I help you?" she asked.

I wondered if she was a good or a bad NPC.

Then she slid down the railway of the stairs, pulled out throwing knives from the bun in her hair and threw them at me. I dodged one, but the other one stabbed into my right shoulder. It went at least two or three inches into my skin, and I roared in pain. I ripped out the knife, and it was the worst pain I'd ever felt in my life. I lifted my rifle and shot her.

Then I started up one of the stairways.

At the top of the stairway were three evil butlers.

I shot them all with the rifle.

Then I was running down the hall, jumping over their bodies.

I could hear the man's voice much more clearly.

It was coming from the door at the far end of this hall. The door was being guarded by two butlers wearing armor of some kind. Like a mixture of knight's armor mixed with futuristic forcefield type of armor.

I stopped, aimed my gun, and sent a spray of bullets into them. The bullets ricocheted off of all their armor with loud noises. After I finished shooting, they started laughing.

Then they started running at me.

I wasn't sure what to do.

I tried unloading a bunch of bullets into them once more. The bullets ricocheted all around, bouncing off into the wooden walls on either side. The men continued coming at me. They were powered up or something. I didn't know what to do, had no ideas.

I started running away from them.

When I got to the far end of the hall, they stopped chasing me and just stood there in the hall. They weren't going to let me past. But I needed to get to that door to help the man.

Sure, I didn't technically need to help him.

But, it was like Dev had said, it could help us. It could give us some more information. I hoped it would give us something good, because we were running out of time. This castle would be underwater any minute now.

How did I know?

Because another tidal wave sounded off.

And then there was that problem: how were we going to get out of this mansion and swim through the water without dying?

The two men were carrying long swords.

I tried shooting them again.

Nothing happened.

One of them yelled at me: "I'm going to cut your head off, kid."

But then Dev and my team showed up at the top of the stairs. Dev was carrying a laser gun, like something you might see in *Star Wars*.

"Dev!" I yelled. "Maybe your gun will work."

He stepped into the hall and fired at the guys. At first, the lasers didn't work, but then the men fell to their knees, crying out in pain. Dev continued firing until they fell flat on their faces. Fried.

We ran past them to the door at the far end.

"Did you guys find anything good?"

"A few things," said Julie.

Then we opened the door.

7

The old man was sitting there in the center of the room in a chair. His hands and legs were duck-taped to the chair so he couldn't get up. He was dressed nice, had gray hair, and looked like a professor.

"Oh, thank goodness you're here," he said.

"Do you know us?" Dev asked.

"No, but I'm sure you're here to help."

"What's up with this place, old man?" Gavin said, looking around the room, holding his gun at the man.

"You can lower your gun," I said. To the old man: "Don't mind him."

The room was the main master bedroom of the house.

It was palatial, had a big bed with a canopy on one side, had all kinds of gold decorations all around. And it had a large painted portrait of the old man who was sitting right here.

"This is your castle?" I asked him.

"Yes. And it's flooding," he said. "I knew this would happen one day."

"You did?" asked Julie.

I went to the man and started cutting away the tape with my knife. As I cut it, my shoulder was screaming in pain. I glanced down at it. Blood was dripping down my entire arm.

Julie noticed. "We need to bandage that up." To the old man, "Do you have a First-Aid kit?"

"In the bathroom," he said, nodding to one side of the room.

Julie took off that direction.

"I have a hot air balloon on the rooftop of this castle. I was on my way to it when my butlers turned against me, tied me to this chair. I don't know what's gotten into them. Well, I do know. And that's why I need to get to that air balloon."

"What do you mean you know what's gotten into them?"

"The spell. That old wizard cast a spell over this entire island, trying to destroy it."

I recalled that information from the orientation video.

"Are you the one?" I asked. "The one who can stop it?"

"Yes," he said. Then his face and his entire presence turned grave. He looked into my eyes, then looked away. It was weird. I thought I recognized him; or had seen him somewhere. "But we have to move fast," he said. "Time is running out. What's more, there's nothing I can do about it without my daughter's help. And she's missing. Was kidnapped by a team sent from that demented wizard."

"How can we help?"

I finished cutting him out of the chair.

"Oh, but you can," the old man said. "You can restore everything. Fix the island, turn back the tides—literally."

"And metaphorically," said Dev.

The old man winked at Dev.

Julie was back now with the bandages. She went to work on my arm.

"If you find my daughter and bring her to me, we can work out the equation that will save the world."

"No big deal," Julie said sarcastically.

"What about you? Where will we find you?"

"I'll be at the beach on the west side of the island. Pacific Peaks. I have a cabin on the top of the hill up there. In the snow. It's the tallest mountain on the island and will be the last place to flood. It's also where the reverse spell will have to be cast."

"Got it," said Dev.

The old man stood and stretched out. "It's our only chance at surviving."

"How do we find your daughter?" I asked.

"Follow the clues. The gang that the wizard contracted is foolish. They've left accidental clues throughout the island. Follow those, save my daughter. Bring her to me."

"Or," said Gavin from across the room, "We can just win the Battle Royale and win the game that way. We don't have to save his daughter or the island. Only ourselves."

But I knew Gavin was wrong.

We had to save the man's daughter.

We had to find the clues.

And we had to not die from the eight hundred Battle Royale fighters.

"We can do this," I muttered to myself.

"What?" Julie asked.

"Before we help you to the balloon, do you have any supplies you can give us?" I asked the old man.

He smiled, led us across his large room to a closet. It was powered by a combination lock. As he entered the digits, he explained, "I keep a vast variety of supplies in case of attack. I never thought it would actually happen." The door slid open. "I have suits for you all. One-size-fits-all. Future tech. You'll be pleased."

We followed him into the closet—which was bigger than Dev's giant room back at home.

There were tons of suits along one of the walls. Military types.

He explained, "These suits are naturally bullet proof with built-in shields. That doesn't mean you can get shot an infinite amount of times. Eventually the bullets will pierce the suit. But they do help. And they look cool."

He was right.

They did look cool.

I selected one off the wall, then went behind a partition in the closet and changed. Everyone selected their own outfits. Julie was wearing cargo shorts and one of the special jackets. I was wearing camouflage pants and a long-sleeved shirt with a handkerchief around my neck. I had a big utility belt that fit perfectly. It had grenades—different types.

The old man also had potions that he gave to Dev. He

explained them to Dev. Some of the potions were meant for healing, some were meant for power-ups. I only overheard bits of their conversation, because I took Gavin aside.

He was wearing a tank top that showed off his muscles. I was glad he was on our team for that very reason. He was tough and bold.

"You're strong. We need you. We can make a great team," I said to him. "But I need you to be a team player."

"Nah," he said.

"I'm the one who should be mad at you," I said.

"Whatever," he said, and pushed past me.

I rolled my eyes.

I went up to the old man. We were ready. Almost.

"Is there room for us in the hot air balloon?" I asked.

"Unfortunately, no."

Gavin said some angry things.

"How do we get out of here?"

"In the downstairs garage, there is a boat. A nice one: Chevy Malibu. Very fast."

"The downstairs is flooded," I said.

"No duh, smart alec," Gavin said.

The old man shrugged.

"What's your name?" I asked him.

"They call me 'The Professor,'" he said. "Help me save the world."

He was an NPC for sure.

They repeated things sometimes.

All I was thinking, however, was how the heck were we supposed to get out of here?

8

We followed The Professor up a back set of stairs to the rooftop of his home. It was windy out here, and dark. Clouds were covering up the sun. The air was harsh—salty.

I could hear the sea monsters growling and making all kinds of ferocious noises all around us. From here, at the tippy-top of the giant castle, we got a great view of the surrounding land. Which wasn't actually land anymore. It was just ocean.

"What the heck?" Gavin said, to himself pretty much.

There was a hot air balloon strapped to the roof.

The Professor climbed into it, turned it on, started

cutting the ties that held it down.

"What's the first clue?" I asked. "To find your daughter."

He took something out of his pocket and tossed it to me.

It was a small GPS, and in it were programmed coordinates.

I figured we had to go to those coordinates. Simple enough. Then The Professor released the balloon from the roof and took off into the sky.

Looking around I realized it really wouldn't be simple at all.

I showed Dev the GPS.

"How far away is that location?" I asked.

There were more planes in the sky, above the clouds, flying over the island. Not all the players had been dropped yet.

I heard motor boats in the distance, more inland, moving away from here. We were way too far out. Needed to get out of here fast.

"We're going to die before the mission even starts," I said with a smirk.

"Don't talk like that," said Julie.

"I was joking. We'll get out of this."

"How?" she asked.

Dev finished his calculations. "It's a good distance. Far inland. Will probably take us a good hour to get there. Maybe more. Depends."

"We need the boat," I said. "That's really our only option."

Gavin smirked now. "How do you suppose we get that?"

"You and I are going for a swim. Down to the garage."

"We're not really going to save that girl, are we?" asked Gavin.

They all looked at me.

"We definitely are. It's smarter than facing seven hundred ninety-six others."

"Minus the four that died from the tidal wave," Dev said.

"Seven hundred ninety-two."

The sound of thunder!

Another tidal wave was headed this way.

And this next tidal wave would cover the entire castle.

To Gavin, I yelled, "We gotta go." To Julie and Dev, I said, "Stay here."

But I could see the giant wave was sweeping this way, to this roof. It would sweep Julie and Dev up with it and they would die. For sure.

"We'll wait inside," said Julie.

"Good idea."

"It'll flood fast, so hurry," she said.

"Got it," I said.

Gavin went to Julie, pulled her close in his arms and kissed her on the lips. A pang of jealousy hit my heart. Gavin told her, "I'll always protect you."

"Let's go," I said to Gavin, then I made eye contact with Julie.

How could she like Gavin so much?

She looked away from me.

"You'll need these," said Dev. "I anticipated this might happen and grabbed them from The Professor's closet." He handed us each a flashlight.

Then Gavin and I were running pell-mell down the stairs. We reached the inner hallways of the house. I was carrying my rifle. Saw a few evil butlers and maids along the way and killed them easily. They were like "easy" level NPCs, apparently.

Then we made it to the third floor. The water had filled up to this floor, like a giant pool. It was dark because the house was dark. I switched on my flashlight, hoping it was waterproof.

Without hesitation, I dove headfirst into the water.

The flashlight helped me see perfectly. Even though it was saltwater, I kept my eyes open. Salt was good for the eyes anyways. I'd taken a deep breath to hold it.

We needed to get all the way to the garage.

I could only hold my breath for two minutes tops.

For the first thirty seconds, I grabbed onto the stair railing and carried myself downwards as fast as I could. Then made it to the main foyer where we'd originally entered.

A body entered my field of vision, making me jump.

I shined my light over.

It was Petrov's dead body.

I saw the big open double doors at the front of the

house. And a shark coming right through it!

10

The shark was just as wide as the doorway, and really long. Since I'd shined my light at it, it opened its mouth and was swimming towards me.

Losing some of my breath from shock and fear, I swam as fast as I could away from the monster. I didn't know where the garage was, but I did know I didn't want to be anywhere near this shark. Gavin was swimming beside me.

We went down a tight hall, which was good because the shark wouldn't be able to fit between the walls. We were swimming faster than ever. The shark tried to come after us, but got stuck.

We continued down this hall, looking through all the open doors, hoping the garage was through one of the doors. I could tell I was starting to lose my breath.

It had been a minute.

I could hear Dev and Julie talking into the ear chip. They'd gone back into the mansion and were in The Professor's room. They were saying that water was crashing in through the windows. The tidal wave had broken all the windows.

"It's flooding fast!" Julie said. "Hurry up, guys."

I saw a green glow.

A second later I saw a long slithering thing only a few feet beneath me. I knew what it was instantly: an electric eel.

It was shimmering with green electricity.

It had been a minute and fifteen seconds.

I swam past a door, shining my light through it, hoping the eel wasn't going to swim upwards and shock me to death. It swam upwards, towards me.

Instantly, I paddled backwards, trying to dodge it, trying to get out of the way. I heard gunfire and saw Gavin shooting at the eel. He unloaded his shotgun a few times. The eel made screeching noises and swam away.

Thank you!

Through this nearest doorway I saw the garage with the boat.

My heart rate doubled in happiness, which was bad because the faster one's heart beats the more oxygen their body needs. And I already needed oxygen really badly.

Swimming towards the boat, all I could think was that I hoped it had a key.

"The room is gonna fill up any moment now," Julie

said, sounding calm.

"I don't know how she's so calm," Dev yelled into the ear chip. "I'm freakin' out. We're gonna drown. We're gonna have to swim out the window."

"We'll be fine," said Julie. "Have faith."

"Please! Go! Faster!" yelled Dev. Then he yelled, "Shark! Through the window! Shark!"

There were keys in the boat, in the ignition, but not turned. I turned it and the boat turned on, fortunately. I was surprised it worked even though it was completely submerged in water. But I wasn't about to question it.

Gavin found the garage door button and clicked it. The sliding door began to open. I put the boat into drive and pushed the throttle forward. It went forward a little but got stuck. I looked around. It was still hooked up to the trailer. I swam around to where it was hooked up and tried to release it. It was like a crank. I wasn't strong enough. I pulled as hard as I could.

Gavin arrived next to me and took my place.

It took him two tries, but he got it undone.

I was in the cockpit now, pushing the throttle forward. He climbed into the nose of the boat. Once he was in, I pushed the throttle all the way forward. We shot out of the garage.

Once out from under the ceiling, the water was nice and bright from the sun. But there were crazy looking sea creatures all around, including a whale just in front of us. I turned the wheel sharply to the right to dodge the whale, but another great white shark entered my view.

I swung the wheel the other way.

We were slowly rising towards the surface. I couldn't

control that. I could only control left or right and forward. Bubbles were releasing from my mouth. I wanted to gulp for air, but I held as strong as I could.

Please, God. Please, God. Please, God, I prayed. Hoping against hope that we'd make it to the surface without getting killed by a sea creature.

11

Our boat surfaced.

The moment it did, I took in a deep breath, taking some water in with the air. I coughed a lot. Coughed up some water, too. But it was nice to be able to breathe.

I swung the boat in a circle, headed towards the rooftop of the mansion, which I couldn't see because the house was completely submerged.

I couldn't see Julie or Dev anywhere.

"Julie!" I yelled into the ear chip. "Dev!"

Gavin was yelling as well.

I went towards where I thought the top of the mansion was. That's when I saw their two bodies pop up out of the water. I pulled up beside them.

Gavin grabbed Julie's hand, pulled her into the boat.

When he went to grab Dev's hand, Dev let out a shriek and then got yanked super fast under the water. One of the sea monsters had grabbed him and sucked him under the water.

"Dev!" I yelled, moving to that side of the boat and peering into the water.

I couldn't see him anywhere.

I grabbed my pistol from the back of my pants and dove headfirst into the water. The sun was out and shining again. I could see clearly under the water, at least twenty feet down, but I couldn't see Dev. Plus, my eyes were starting to sting from the salt now.

I kept swimming as fast as I could anyway, straight down.

It started to get dark and my ears were burning from the water pressure. I started losing my air, looking everywhere for Dev. Stupidly, I'd forgotten my flashlight.

I couldn't see him anywhere.

I kept swimming.

My mind took me back to just half an hour ago when we'd been watching that orientation video, when Petrov had still been alive. I remembered being a little happy about getting dropped off onto a Battle Royale island. I was slightly in doubt at the time. I didn't think it would be real. I thought it would be like laser tag or something.

This was not what I had expected.

I didn't like it anymore.

I wanted to get off the island.

Not because I was afraid. I'm not a scaredy-cat. I don't back away from fights. But for the sake of my friends, I wanted off.

I kept swimming.

If Dev or Julie died on my watch, I wouldn't be able to live with myself. Petrov himself had said it: *I was the leader*. That was the thing, though. I didn't want to be the leader. I didn't want to be responsible. Even if he hadn't said I was the leader, I would have taken charge because I would want to protect my friends. I would die for my friends. Easily. Without even a second thought.

But I couldn't promise them or myself that I could keep them safe. There was too much that could go wrong. I was beginning to understand this island. And it terrified me.

Petrov was dead.

Which meant that Dev or Julie could die.

I kept swimming.

I was half out of breath.

I used some breath to yell as loud as I could under the water. "Dev!"

I stopped swimming, listened.

No response.

I saw a glowing green eel coming towards me. I raised my pistol and shot it a few times. It screeched and slithered away.

Then I saw a shark appear only ten feet from me. Its mouth was gaping wide open and its white pointy teeth glistened. I aimed for its mouth, fired three shots, then swam upwards as fast as I could.

That's when I heard a scream under the water.

Twenty feet below me—

I started swimming for it.

I probably only had ten percent breath left, but I knew

it had to be Dev.

It was dark.

I got ten feet further down.

It was too dark.

I wouldn't be able to see a shark if it was coming at me.

When I got ten more feet down, I could see Dev. He was pinned against the floor of the ocean—which was a green lawn, the one we'd been on in front of the mansion. Something was tied around his foot. Somehow he'd gotten connected to something heavy. I couldn't see what it was. I whipped out my knife and started cutting away at it.

He was making noises.

He was going to drown if I didn't get him to the surface fast.

Heck, I was going to drown if I didn't get us up there fast.

Hold on, buddy, was all I was thinking.

I cut at the ropes around his ankles. Super confused at what I was even cutting. Because it was really dark. I could tell it was loosening.

Finally, after what felt like forever, I got his foot loose.

Grabbing him by the shirt, I started kicking upwards.

He started swimming with me. I let go of him and we pulled towards the surface as fast and hard as we could. As if our lives depended on it, because they freakin' did.

Again, my mind flashed back to when we were in the plane on the freeway, preparing for takeoff. Again, I realized I should have been more like Julie. I should have questioned what this was all about. I should have tried to get out of it. This wasn't worth it. My friends' lives in danger wasn't worth it.

Battle Royale is not that fun in real life.
At all.

12

Dev and I made it back to the boat.

It was kind of like that expression, though: out of the frying pan, into the fire. We were all safe in the boat. "Safe" being the relative word.

It was weird.

I took my seat behind the wheel and started throttling us forward, through the water. And for the first minute or two, everything was calm. Or so it seemed.

There were no sea monsters around that we could see.

We moved peacefully over the water.

Looking over the side of the boat, I could see the tops of trees just ten feet beneath us. We were over the top of the forest I'd seen earlier. Moving inland.

I got us up to top speed.

The wind was blowing through our hair.

Everything around us was pretty peaceful.

I'd thought for sure a giant squid was going to attack us.

Julie was next to me in the co-pilot's seat.

"I thought for sure a giant squid was going to attack us," I yelled to her.

I shouldn't have said that.

You can probably guess what happened next.

A GIANT SQUID ATTACKED US!

13

It happened only five seconds after I'd made the statement. A giant tentacle, wider than our boat, shot up out of the water just beside us and fell over the back end of the boat, almost taking out Dev and Gavin, who were sitting back there. Gavin was instantly on his feet. He had one foot in the boat. One foot on the edge of the boat. He had the bazooka over his shoulder and he was firing away into the water. Spamming the water.

"Sketch!" yelled Dev.

I figured he was talking about the giant squid situation, but I glanced back and saw Dev pointing at something off to our right. There was a giant boat, a sea boat (whereas ours was a small and fast lake boat), coming towards us. Fast.

Another team.

"Battle Royale, baby," I said under my breath.

I kept our path forward as the boat came at us from the right. They were a few hundred yards off.

"Watch out for the snipes," said Dev.

"How?" I yelled.

"I don't know," he said.

"Duck a lot," said Gavin.

I was seated in the front of the boat, behind the wheel. How was I supposed to duck? Julie slinked down in her seat as far as she could go. I slinked down as far as I could go and still see out the windshield. I hoped to gosh they didn't have sniper rifles.

Just then, a rocket launched from their boat, coming towards us.

14

The giant squid was nowhere to be seen.

But a freakin' rocket was coming towards us. I was calm, focused. Like how I usually am when I'm in fights; and I've been in a lot of fights. I had the wheel. I was in control. We'd get this done.

Instead of dodging the rocket by veering away from the boat, I yanked the wheel around, bringing us into a hard right. Right towards the sea boat.

They were bigger, but we were faster, could maneuver more easily.

I sliced across the water towards them. Our boat, because of its angle, was casting a wall of water off to one side.

The rocket passed over our heads.

They fired another rocket.

But Gavin fired one of his.

It was crazy, because I saw it happen. Two seconds after each rocket was fired they collided with each other in midair. A giant explosion lit up that area of the sky.

I kept the wheel to the right, for the rival team.

Gavin fired more rockets.

Julie remained hidden.

Dev was looking at the GPS for some reason.

Three of Gavin's rockets hit their boat broadside, blasting it to pieces, overturning it, causing waves and fire and embers and all kinds of debris.

I continued toward it, because we would need to make sure the team was completely dead. And we would need to loot them for supplies.

I slowed our approach.

I heard the next TIDAL WAVE sound off far behind us. It would reach us in about a minute probably. We would be able to ride the wave. I hoped.

"Four down," said Gavin, standing in the space in the front of the boat between Julie and I.

"Good job," said Julie.

"That was good, Gavin," I said.

We reached the boat, holding our rifles at the ready, aiming into the floating wreckage. I saw one dead guy laying over some scrap metal. Dev sent a few shots into him just in case. I saw one guy clambering for a different piece of floating metal. I shot him a few times. Then I piloted the boat directly through the middle of the flaming wreckage. The flames were small and dying by this point.

Gavin found some bazooka rockets.

That was about it.

I left the wreckage and took us inland. Dev pointed to where I needed to go. We were going to the coordinates The Professor had given us. To save his daughter. To save the world.

"Nothing to it," Gavin said. "We can win this. We can win the Battle Royale."

I agreed. But I knew we needed all the advantage we could get. Which is why I followed the coordinates. The Tidal Wave reached us and took us high into the sky and then rolled out from under us. It gave us a speed boost.

I kept us aimed directly towards the coordinates.

Fifteen minutes passed.

During that time, I hadn't seen or heard any additional planes. All the players were on the island now. Finally, after thirty minutes of traveling, seeing no one, and nothing happening, we reached the place where the water ended and the land began. Of course, the water would keep moving inland.

But we could finally get off the boat.

We had no choice.

15

We hiked for two hours, through a thick forest, over a mountain. It was getting dark beyond the trees. The sun was setting fast. Faster than it did normally.

We didn't see another living soul for the entire two hours.

Then the sun was down.

We were still in the forest and couldn't see the end of it. Practically the whole way Gavin had argued with me. "We should just fight," he said. "We can loot, build, fortify. I'm good at this. We'll win. Trust me."

"Trust me," I said. "I know we need to do this."

"How do you know?" he asked.

"I just know."

Julie didn't interject into our arguments.

Julie and Gavin walked twenty feet behind us for some time, talking amongst each other and I couldn't hear what they were saying.

Then, at one point, Julie was walking beside me while Gavin and Dev lagged twenty feet behind.

"Are you sure you're doing the right thing?" she asked. "I trust you. But do you know what you're doing?"

I wasn't sure. But I needed to be confident, especially in front of her. "I am sure," I said. In my imagination, I was back on my rooftop, crying that night my parents first told me they were getting divorced. I'd been shattered. I'd never truly recovered. And I'd never been sure about anything since. Except that I was somebody.

I had to be.

Right?

The aliens didn't come and get me, nothing extraordinary had happened to me that night, but I'd worked hard the last few years. I'd learned lots of skills. I worked hard in school. I was popular. I had everything but the car and the girl.

These were all justifications—these were all things I told myself to make myself feel important, like I mattered. But I wasn't sure if I did.

And I wasn't sure why Petrov had put me in charge.

"This can't be real," said Julie. "It has to be a dream, right?"

I was shaking my head. "No."

"How do you know?" she asked.

"Because in my dreams, and in my daydreams, I—" I stopped for a moment. I was afraid to say it and my heart was beating out of my chest. But I had to say it.

I'd been holding it in my heart for too long.

Julie was so pretty, even now after all the crazy stuff that had happened. Her crazy blue highlights were wet and stuck to her face. She looked small and cute and frail beside me, like someone I needed to protect. I knew, though, that she was strong and capable. More than most girls. That was for sure.

I wanted to tell her I liked her.

This wasn't a dream.

I knew this was REAL for many reasons.

Because it was real, I was very afraid of losing my friends, of them dying. Which meant I needed to tell Julie the truth about how I felt.

"How do you know it's not a dream?" she asked.

My hands were sweaty, now, just thinking about what I was going to say next. My mouth was going dry. I wasn't sure I would be able to talk. To get the words out.

I went for it.

"I know it's not a dream," I said, "because in my dreams you're my girlfriend. And, out here, you're not." I didn't want to tell her this, but in my dreams of Julie we always ended up kissing.

I didn't dare look at her.

What was her reaction going to be?

16

Julie didn't respond to me for a few seconds. I decided I would look at her face. I was wondering what she was thinking. Before I turned, she punched me in the shoulder.

"You're sometimes really stupid, Allen, you know that?"

Then she punched me again.

"You're not stupid. You're just a jerk, actually."

Then she dropped back to the others.

I was by myself for a few moments until Dev ran up to catch up.

"So, how'd it go?" he asked.

I was shocked, offended, and a little mad. "What the

heck's wrong with her?" I said.

"It didn't go good?"

Not good at all. "Remember, Dev, that one sleepover when you said that girls are impossible to understand?"

"Yeah?"

"I didn't believe you. Now I do." Under my breath, I muttered, "How am I the jerk?"

I didn't dare glance back at her and Gavin. How could she call me a jerk, but then like Gavin? He was an ultra jerk.

Before I could think much of it, the sun was totally and completely down. The forest was dark. I flicked on my flashlight and took the lead.

"If a team sees our lights, they can easily pick us off."

Dev had a point.

"We have no choice," I said.

"We always have a choice."

"Why do you think Petrov left me as the team leader?" I asked.

"Isn't it obvious?" he said.

"Not at all."

Before Dev could explain, we heard a growling noise from a nearby animal. I stopped, shined my light all around. I couldn't tell where the noise was coming from. Gavin and Julie joined us. We stood in a circle, flashing our lights all around.

I had my pistol in one hand.

Flashlight in the other.

"We need to get out of this forest," said Dev.

"We could run," I said.

"We could fight," Gavin said.

"We can do both," said Julie.

"I'm with Julie," said Dev.

"On three," I said. But, instead of counting down, I just said, "Actually, NOW!"

We booked it through the forest, running as fast as we could. I heard more growls, from all sides, and howls. There were evil creatures in this forest for sure. It was hard running in the complete darkness through a tangle of forest. We had to jump over logs, duck under branches, get smacked in the face by branches.

After sprinting for ten minutes straight, we got to the end of the forest and exited it without having to fight any evil wolves.

Outside the forest was a steep hill.

At the bottom of the hill was a gigantic—and I mean gigantic—spaceship. It was parked on a giant concrete lot, surrounded by tall buildings that looked like an abandoned space station.

Now that we were outside the forest and felt safe, Dev was looking at the GPS.

"Almost there," he said. "The coordinates lead to that space station." Dev looked down at the GPS, then down to the space station. "Apparently."

I shrugged.

"Am I the only one who thinks it's pretty crazy to randomly see a giant space station?" Gavin said.

"Death Island is full of surprises," said Julie.

17

"Why would the girl be in the space station?" asked Julie. "And how do we know it's her?"

We were walking down the large slope towards the station. The moon and stars were bright overhead. We could barely hear the growls from the monsters back in the forest.

And it was cold. The wind was blowing, and I couldn't wait to get inside the station. Other than the wind and the background growling sounds, the night was quiet.

We didn't need our flashlights.

I couldn't see or hear any sound of any other teams in this area. There were hundreds of us on the island, but it was a huge island. I wondered how many people were still left alive.

We were walking side by side, the four of us, not really talking.

Julie wasn't even looking at me.

I wondered what was going through her crazy girl head. How could girls be so emotional and crazy? Maybe it was the blue hair dye. Maybe it was seeping into her brain.

I smiled to myself, even though that wasn't even funny.

"Why are you smiling?" she asked me.

I was shocked that she'd spoken to me.

"No reason," I said.

"Tell me," she said.

"Later," I said.

"Jerk," she said, but this time she said it more jokingly, as if she was apologizing for earlier. In a way. Those were the last words any of us spoke as we walked to the station.

We were pretty tired.

At least, I was.

All of my equipment was heavy.

My backpack and guns and ammo.

Dev was carrying the heaviest pack, filled with ammo. I looked at him. He was struggling. His face was really sweaty. But he was keeping up, despite the fact that he wasn't athletic.

It would all be over soon, I told myself.

We'd find the girl in the space station.

We'd bring her to the beach.

We'd save the world.

Nothing to it.

Boy was I wrong.

Because there, in the space station, is where everything fell completely apart. Some things happen so fast you can barely even react. That's kind of how it was.

18

It should have been a simple mission. The space station was quiet, deserted. There was no one we could see. Little did we know that we were walking into an ambush.

We followed the GPS coordinates to the building that surrounded the spaceship. The spaceship was gigantic— bigger than Dev's house. Probably five or six of Dev's mansion houses put together. It was the kind of spaceship you see in space shows or movies. The kind of ship that a crew of thousands could live on for months at a time. A giant square skyscraper building was built around the ship in a giant square. Thus, the ship was in an open courtyard.

The building was basically like an airport.

And that's what it looked like on the inside.

Like an empty airport terminal. If you've ever been in one you know what I'm talking about. The floors were cold and shiny. Swept and clean. There were lots of shops all around, like China Panda, Dippin' Dots, Hot Dog on a Stick, all closed. There were offices in some of the wings, where the space station's techs worked. Or used to work.

The place looked like it hadn't been used in a long time.

The place had giant windows made of glass and the moonlight shone through, bouncing off the shiny floors. As such, we didn't need to use our flashlights.

We walked quietly, being as careful as possible.

When all of the sudden, the lights started turning on.

Then an alarm sounded.

"Where are we supposed to go to find the girl?" I yelled over the alarm sounds, concerned about what was going to happen next.

"I think she's in the spaceship," said Dev.

"Let's get her."

As we ran through the terminal building and made it to the courtyard where the spaceship was, I saw a group of astronauts. Yes, you heard me right. Astronauts. They were wearing the typical astronaut space suits and they were running towards us from the right. They were also wielding laser rifles. Four of them.

They lifted their guns.

"Intruders!" they yelled, and they started shooting at us.

We returned fire, but we had no cover because we were in the open courtyard. The spaceship was fifty yards out.

"To the ship," I yelled.

I shot as I ran. I couldn't tell if I was hitting any of the astronauts. But two of them went down by the time we reached a stairway that apparently entered the ship.

The inside of the ship looked how you would expect— long futuristic looking corridors, slightly rounded. Everything was polished and shiny. Lights turned on in response to movement as I ran down the corridor.

"Directions?" I yelled to Dev.

"You're going the right way."

I could hear the loud alarms from the terminal.

I turned a corner of the corridor and saw TWENTY evil astronauts at the far end, running down towards us. I turned back from the corridor.

"Back!" I yelled.

My team and I booked it back from where we'd come from.

Problem was, more evil astronauts were coming from that way now. At least TWENTY more. Like, jeez. I dropped to the ground to make myself a smaller target and started blasting the guys. Their spacesuits made them harder to kill. You had to shoot them more to knock them down.

We were all unloading fire. Meanwhile the other group of TWENTY was getting closer, about to close in on us. We were pinned. With no cover. There were no doors anywhere near us. We were effectively stuck. And then my clip ran out and I needed to reload. Gavin was spamming all his weapons at one of the groups.

"We're too exposed!" yelled Dev.

Just when I thought we had no hope, I heard a grenade explode. I turned around to see the astronauts to our back were dying. Getting shot at from behind. I was confused.

We finished off the twenty in front of us.

The ones behind us were finished off within seconds. Then eight astronauts in space suits stepped into the open. The ones who'd killed the one group for us. They weren't shooting at us.

"Who are you?" I asked.

The guy in the lead, a tall guy, took off his space helmet. "The good astronauts," he said.

"Do you know where the girl is?" I asked.

"The Professor's daughter? Of course," he said.

He was tall, had long wavy hair. Didn't look very old. Maybe sixteen at the most.

"Aren't you a little young to be an astronaut?" Julie asked.

"Aren't you a little young to be playing Battle Royale?"

She shrugged.

"Follow us," the guy said.

We did.

19

They led us to the command room of the spaceship—the part of the spaceship where you could fly the ship. There were panels of computers against the walls. There was an actual steering wheel in the center of the room. The room was huge.

And there was a young girl, around our age, looking out the front window. I couldn't see her face, but from the way she was standing she seemed sad.

The eight astronauts parted so that we could walk through to the girl. "Emma," the lead astronaut said, the good looking one.

"Thanks," I said.

We walked across the room. When we were halfway to her, she looked back at us. Seemed scared at first.

"We know your dad," I said. "He needs your help."

That seemed to make her less alarmed, but then her face went sad and she looked out the window once more.

When I finally reached her, she wouldn't look at me.

There wasn't much to see out the window.

"We're here to bring you to your dad," I said. "To rescue you."

"That's very kind," she said, still not looking at me. "Sadly, I'm not the one that needs rescuing."

That's when she looked at me. Her hair was long and brown. Moonlight fell across one side of her face and I saw that she was my age and that she was beautiful.

I gulped.

"What do you mean?"

"She means this," said the lead astronaut—the one with the wavy hair. He pressed a button on his spacesuit and it fell off. The others did as well. They were dressed like us.

That's when I realized it.

They weren't NPCs.

They were Battle Royale players.

Real people.

They lifted their guns at us to kill us.

20

I felt stupid. Why did I trust the fake astronauts? Whatever. I didn't want to die. So I tried to get these "astronauts" to talk. To stall them so I could figure out a plan. There was eight of them and only four of us and they had much more gun power than we did. That was for sure.

"What's your name?" I asked the lead one.

"Liam," he said.

"I'm Allen."

"Nice to meet you. Girl with the purple hair," he said.

"It's blue," Julie said.

"Doesn't matter. What's your name?" he asked.

"Doesn't matter," she said, holding her pistol out at him now.

"Don't shoot, darling. I'll blow your face off. And all of your friends to bits."

"Then do it," she said.

My jaw was tight. Why was Julie egging them on?

She had a point though. Why weren't they just shooting us?

"We want to make a trade," he said.

"What kind of trade?"

"Why's there eight of you?" Gavin interrupted. "The squads are only four."

"Two squads teamed up," Dev said. "They're some kind of clan. Which is probably against the rules."

"There are no rules," said Liam.

"What do you want, Liam?" I asked.

"I want the girl for the girl. We'll let you have Emma. You can take her to The Professor and you can save the world. We want the girl with the blue hair."

I was shocked. Why did they want Julie? It didn't even make sense.

"No way," I said.

"I have a name," said Julie. And she said her name. "Why me?" she asked.

"You're not taking her," said Gavin.

"For sure not," I said.

"Listen," Liam said. "It's a fair trade."

"But why me?" asked Julie.

"The Wizard told us to bring the girl with the blue hair to him. And we would win."

"The Wizard who cast the spell over Death Island?" I asked. "That guy is evil. And probably lying to you."

"Maybe," Liam said. "But he also said we'd get rich if we brought her to him. And he's not lying." Liam took a few gold coins from his pocket, held them up. "The man already gave us a down payment. He showed us the gold, too. Enough that me and my boys would never have to work a day in our lives again. We will be rich."

"Look," said Dev, "obviously this Wizard guy is bad. Not to be trusted. This island is similar to a video game, and I've played enough video games to know that you should never make a deal with the devil. And that's essentially who this wizard is."

"No, he's not. He's a scientist. They just call him a wizard because he's really good at science. He has a huge laboratory on the east side. When they say he 'cast a spell,' that's just lingo. He actually has a giant machine that can control the weather and the oceans and the sea. All that kind of stuff."

"Still," I said. "He's not a good guy."

"But he's rich."

"Money isn't everything," Julie said.

"He probably won't hurt you," Liam said. "He just said to bring you to him alive."

Julie put a gun to her own head. "I'll shoot myself if you don't lower your weapons."

Liam instantly lowered his. "Whoa," he said. "Calm down, Julie."

"We're not trading," I said, realizing Julie was just making a play. I knew she wouldn't actually shoot herself. She was too much of a survivalist.

I noticed that Dev was slowly moving a few feet to his left, toward one of the spaceship's control panels. I wondered if any of the others were noticing.

"It's not just for the money," said Liam. "It's for what the money can buy." He became solemn. "It's for my mom. She's dying. We're poor and can't afford the medical bills."

I bought the story for one second.

Until Dev said, "You're not poor. I recognize you. You're a *Fortnite* streamer. You have over a million subs. I'm subbed to you. You're rich."

He smiled, scoffed. "You got me," he said.

Before he could say anything else, Dev hit a button on the control panel and the spaceship powered on with a booming noise. Gavin started shooting at the astronauts, causing them to jump for cover. I jumped behind a panel for cover. Emma crouched beside me. So did the others. Except for Gavin, who was going nuts on the guns. He killed three of the eight enemy team so far.

"You're making a mistake," I heard Liam yell.

I turned around, getting a sudden idea.

"Toss me your rocket launcher!" I yelled to Gavin.

I didn't know if this was a good idea, but it was worth a shot. He tossed it. I caught it and, without thinking or slowing down, I aimed it directly at the front glass windshield. I shot a rocket through it and the glass shattered to pieces, creating a large opening. We could escape from this room. The front of the ship sloped downwards out the window. We could slide down it and fall the final twenty feet to the grass under the ship.

I took Emma's hand. "We need to go. We need to get you to your dad."

That's when Gavin took a big bullet to the stomach. It knocked him out the open window and he slid back down it, yelling in pain as he fell.

"I can cure that," shouted Dev. "Hold your ground."

We were ducked down behind the control panel, which was probably going to break soon from the amount of bullets these guys were sending into it.

I was still holding Emma's hand.

Julie was looking into my eyes. "Save Gavin," she said. "You don't know him like I do."

She had a tear in her eye.

I was confused.

Bullets were still pounding into the panel.

"We outnumber you," said Liam. "Give up. Give us Julie and we'll leave you alone. We'll let you live. And, who knows, maybe The Wizard will let Julie live."

Julie was crouched right next to me. She kissed me on the cheek. "I trust you," she said. Then she squeezed my arm. "I have feelings for you, Allen. And now I need *you* to trust me."

She was planning on surrendering herself.

"Take Emma to her dad."

"No," I yelled to Julie.

But she was headstrong. She didn't give me a chance to object or try to stop her. She stood up, above the panel, raising her arms, throwing down her gun. The shooting stopped. Then she walked around the panel and walked towards Liam's team.

"Stay down," I said to Emma.

And I stood up, holding my rifle out. Dev did the same. I couldn't hear Gavin down below. I hoped he was still alive.

"The girl has some sense," said Liam.

21

I watched Julie walk the rest of the way across the room to Liam and it felt like slow motion to me. I was trying to figure out a plan, a way out of this.

I knew that if he took her and escaped from this place that I would do everything in my power to bring her back. I would do everything I possibly could to get her back.

Then she was standing with them.

Liam was smiling, a playful smile, like he knew something we didn't.

"Go heal Gavin," I said to Dev.

Dev had some of those healing potions. He turned back, jumped out the window. Liam and the gang let him, apparently. They had what they wanted.

Liam took Julie's hand in his and kissed it.

Emma was still crouched beside me.

I didn't care, though. If we lost Julie, why should I care? If they were to take Julie now, I would change my mission to rescue her from The Wizard. I wouldn't care about getting Emma to her father.

Liam's crooked smile turned into a laugh.

Then he spun Julie around so that she was facing me, he held an arm across her neck and put a gun to her head. He was using her as a shield.

"Tricked you," he said.

I didn't understand.

"I made all that up about The Wizard." He was laughing even more now. "I was trying to do this the nice way. All that conversation a minute ago, when you were trying to stall me, I was just trying to get information from you. But, gotta give it to you, you never said it."

"Said what?" I asked.

"Where The Professor is hiding. I want to know his location. Then we can kill him and win this Battle Royale style. As it should be won."

Now everything made sense. The realization slammed into my mind like a ton of bricks. He'd been chatting away with us trying to get information. He knew we were coming here for Emma. Apparently we were the only team coming for Emma—the only team trying to beat the mission non-Battle Royale style. And he wanted to win the Battle Royale.

He was a famous *Fortnite* streamer.

Of course he would want to win the Battle Royale.

"Don't tell him," Julie said. "He's a liar."

"I'll shoot her," said Liam. "I'll do it," he yelled!

"Don't do it, Allen," she yelled. "You're meant to save the island. You can do this. But you can't tell him. Don't tell him."

22

Julie wasn't scared. She usually wasn't scared. She didn't understand what Death Island was all about, but she knew it had something to do with the necklaces around their necks. Perhaps they needed to learn the things that were inscribed on their necklaces.

"I'm going to kill her, Allen," shouted Liam, a voice interlaced with vitriol and anger. Liam really, really wanted to win. Apparently he had a lot to prove.

Julie noticed that none of the guys on these teams had the necklaces, which was strange, because Petrov had said they were the key to everything.

"What happened to your necklaces?" Julie asked.

"What are you talking about?" said Liam.

"Were you not given necklaces?"

"Those stupid things," he yelled. "I threw mine away."

Julie wondered if those who didn't throw away the necklaces were the ones who got chances to meet The Professor and learn how to save the world. Death Island was obviously some sort of experiment. All of these bad guys were teenagers, like them.

"How did you get to the Island?" Julie asked.

"Got detention," said Liam. Then: "Enough talking! Time is running out. The water is going to be here soon. Speak, Allen, or I'll kill her."

Julie was watching Allen's eyes. There was a lot of conflict in them. She could tell that he was about to give it away to Liam.

"I'll be able to tell if you're lying. And I'll kill her," Liam shouted, spit coming from his mouth.

That's when Julie realized something else.

The moment she realized it, her blue necklace turned a bright green.

Allen saw the change. Julie saw it in her peripheral vision. And she knew what she had to do. She just hoped Allen would realize it as well.

23

I aimed my rifle at Liam. Since he was hiding behind Julie, I couldn't get a clear shot. I ran through all the options in my mind. I could try to take this shot, but it was unlikely that I'd hit Liam and more likely that I'd hit Julie. I could try to run across the room, but Liam would easily shoot me. I could give him the location and he might let Julie go, but more likely than not he would just kill her. I was leaning towards giving him the location of The Professor.

The words were on the tip of my tongue when something strange happened. Julie elbowed Liam in the gut. Then, instead of trying to get away, using her free arm, she reached across to where Liam was holding the pistol to her head. She jammed her finger between the trigger guard and Liam's finger. And she pulled the trigger, killing herself.

I couldn't even begin to describe how it looked. There was blood everywhere. I don't like to even think about it. Again, it felt like slow motion to me.

And Julie fell out of Liam's arms, collapsing to the floor in a slump. Dead. Totally and completely dead. Dev's potions wouldn't work because they only worked if the person was still partially alive. But she'd died instantly. She'd shot herself.

I was shocked, confused, angry.

I started firing my rifle at the teams, but there were too many of them. They started spraying back and I had to duck behind the panel with Emma.

"Oh my gosh!" I yelled.

Realizing there was nothing I could do to save Julie, that she was dead, I followed my instincts. I was filled with rage and anger and just wanted to stand up and try to kill these guys and die trying. Instead, I followed the original plan, following some deep gut instincts I didn't even realize I was following.

I crouched around Emma, to the far side of the control panel. To a switch that I'd noticed earlier that I was pretty sure would launch this spaceship upwards.

I reached my hand over the panel, pushing all the buttons.

The spaceship made lots of noises. I could hear the giant engines rumbling. I grabbed Emma's hand and jumped out the front windshield with her, landing down on the metal slope, slipping, and sliding downwards as the ship started to launch skyward.

We fell off the ship with twenty feet under our feet.

I hoped Emma knew how to land.

We landed, bent at the knees and rolled as the ship shot upwards. If the team figured out how to control it, we would be dead meat. They would come back down for us. There were only three of us—not counting Emma since we were trying to protect her—and Gavin was wounded.

I saw Dev leaned over Gavin's body, administering the potion. Gavin was sitting up now, looking at me. "Where's Julie?" he asked.

I didn't know how to respond.

My eyes fell away from him.

I looked to Emma. I didn't care about the mission anymore.

"I'm so sorry," Emma said.

I looked upwards. The ship was still ascending and fast. But I saw small things coming from out of the ship. At first I didn't recognize them, but then I saw that it was the team. They were flying down with jetpacks.

"We need to move," I said.

"Where's Julie?" Gavin yelled, on his feet and coming towards me to fight.

I steeled my jaw.

"Where's Julie?" he roared with such a viciousness that I felt he would kill me. I knew he wouldn't be able to. I was too good at hand-to-hand combat. Something about the way he yelled with such emotion actually showed how much he truly did care about Julie. We both cared very much for her.

"Allen!"

He was within ten feet of me.

Not slowing down.

The team was still flying down overhead.

"Now's not the time," Dev shouted. "We need to get out of here."

"I thought you were the leader! You were supposed to protect us! Save us!"

Gavin lunged at me, throwing out his fist as hard as he could. I easily dodged back. He threw another fist. I dodged to one side. He tried to kick me. I blocked it with my leg.

"Now's not the time," I said. "Gavin."

He continued trying to hit me, so finally I just landed a front kick in his stomach and sent him flying back to the concrete, knocking the wind out of him.

"Gavin!" I yelled.

The team was lowering towards us fast. Already started to send bullets down on us.

Something wasn't right. Julie wouldn't have done that had she not figured something out. Had she not known something I didn't know.

There was something missing.

I needed to think.

My instincts told me to get the heck out of here. To get away from this team. To keep Emma safe. Because there had to be a way.

There had to be a way to get Julie back, right?

Why the heck would she do that?!

Taking Emma's hand, I started running towards the nearest door to the buildings. My adrenaline was coursing through my veins. Heart going wild.

Dev and Gavin followed.

Emma was a slow runner.

"We need a vehicle."

"There're a few Teslas in the backlot," Emma said.

The team landed in the courtyard just as we pushed through the doors to the building. They fired at the windows, breaking all the glass. We ran deeper into the terminal. Unfortunately there were no shadows and I saw a group of evil NPC astronauts to the right.

I glanced back and saw one of the teammates holding a long sniper rifle perfectly steady. Aimed towards Emma and I. He fired. Something in me told me he would hit the target. I didn't know how I'd known. But I had.

A split-second later, the bullet hit Emma in the chest.

And she died, holding my hand.

24

I ran, because that was my only option.

Julie was dead.

Emma was dead.

Everything was a blur. I can barely remember how we got to it, but we got to the Tesla. Dev drove us because Gavin and I were both in a sort of state of shock.

I was in the passenger seat, staring out the window as Dev accelerated to max speed, taking us out of the space station, further inland, over the grassy hills. A tidal wave rushed behind us, trying to catch up, but it had nothing on the Tesla.

I put my face in my hands.

I didn't cry, though I wanted to.
We'd lost everything.
All we had left was the Battle Royale, but I didn't care.

Into Darkness

1

Dev drove us up the nearest mountain. On the other side was what looked like a city of askew skyscrapers. Some of the skyscrapers were a little bent to one side or the other, as if they were leaning. Other than that the place looked very similar to one of those very high-tech and colorful Japanese cities.

There were a lot of NPCs.

And we could hear gunfire coming from the city, which meant that there were probably a lot of teams fighting down there. It would be a hotspot for loot and for death. Plus there were a lot of shops down there. You could buy new outfits, weapons, shields, vehicles, houses, pretty much anything you could think of. I had no interest or reason to go into the city, but Dev drove us towards it.

As I stared into the lights and my vision went blurry, my mind started spinning. Why would Julie have done that? After ten minutes passed, Gavin finally asked. And he sounded calm. — "How did she die?"

I looked back at him.

His eyes were watery.

I felt a new affection for him.

Then, as I recalled the memory of Julie dying, I remembered seeing her blue necklace turn green. Her necklace had said "Strength," on it. Why had it turned green? The three of ours were still blue. Julie had figured something out. The necklaces were important and hers had changed.

"She…" I started to explain, but I didn't have it in me to recount the details.

Besides, there was something very off about how she'd died.

I knew I was missing something.

Had to have been.

I saw a jeep loaded up with a full squad of four a few hundred yards from us, headed into the city. "You sure it's a good idea to go into the city?" I asked Dev.

"You tell me," said Dev. "You're our leader."

Julie had told me to save the island, and that was after she'd decided to kill herself. That was after she'd surrendered. Had she decided to kill herself from the moment she'd surrendered?

Why had the necklace turned green?

And how could I save the island now that Emma was dead as well?

As we entered the city, driving onto one of the busy streets, I figured it out. I figured out why Julie had killed herself.

The street looked very much like a street in New York, packed to the brim with traffic and taxis and shops. Except it was more colorful and futuristic like Japan. Dev drove our car onto the sidewalk, forcing NPC pedestrians to jump out of the way. There was also apparently a "jump" feature on the Tesla, which allowed him to jump over cars and objects. It always hurt when we landed back down, but it was a good feature.

"I guess it's a Tesla Generation 4 or 5," said Dev with a laugh as he jumped a few cars.

The jeep full of squad mates appeared behind us. They started unloading their guns at us, but the Tesla was bullet proof. And Dev was driving fast and surprisingly skillfully. All that time he spent playing racing games in his room was paying off.

"How did she die?" Gavin asked once more.

I turned back to him, a glint in my eye. "We can get her back," I said. "I think there's a way. And we're going to do it."

2

"How?" asked Dev.

"She's dead," said Gavin. "There is no way."

"No. There is a way," I said. "But we're going to need supplies. And a guide."

Just then, Dev screeched our car to a halt beside a store that sold supplies. It was called, THE EMPORIUM. I opened my door, got out. The city was loud. There was an NPC vendor selling hot dogs nearby. I went to him to get one for myself.

"That will be ten credits," he said.

"Will you accept a gun?"

He shrugged.

I gave him one of my pistols. He gave me a hot dog.

It was delicious. I ate it in a few bites as we headed into The Emporium. The Emporium was a three story megastore replete with all the best of the best tech. But, from what I could tell, everything was super expensive. The most expensive thing was on the back wall. An EMP.

I didn't play video games, but I knew what it was.

Electronic Magnetic Pulse.

It's a device that, once pressed, disables all the technology in the surrounding area. It shuts down cars and planes and anything that's electrically powered.

"Actually," said Dev, placing his hand on my shoulder as I was looking up at the EMP, "that's not your typical EMP. It knocks out all power. But it also melts all surrounding metal. Thus, it melts guns. If you hit the EMP, all of the nearby enemies' guns will be worthless. Grenades—worthless. Laser guns. Everything."

"But it's a million credits."

The store manager approached us. "Need help with anything?"

Gavin pointed to the shelves of big guns. "I want some of those."

"How many credits do you have to spend?" the man asked.

"None," I said.

"Then unfortunately we can't serve you."

"How do we get credits?" I asked.

"You have to work for credits. Loot it off of other teams."

"Any other ways?" I asked. We didn't really have time to get jobs or fight a bunch of teams. I was pretty sure there was a way to save Julie, but we'd have to act fast, before the Battle Royale ended. Before she died for reals.

"There is a dance competition."

I smiled. "Nearby?"

The man nodded.

"How many credits if I win?" I asked.

"A million."

"That's enough for the EMP," said Dev.

"We need guns," said Gavin.

"We need a guide," I said. "To the underworld. To save Julie."

3

I didn't have time to explain it all to them. I didn't have time to explain how I'd figured it out because we needed credits AND fast. We didn't really need the EMP, though it seemed it would be cool to have. Didn't really know what we could use it for—what we needed was a guide to the underworld.

Or whatever it was called.

And we would need credits for that.

I didn't know particularly if there was an underworld, but there had to be something like it. There had to be a place where dead people went. Was this island real? Yes. But it didn't work the same as the rest of the world.

Everything was different here.

And I knew that I knew that I knew that Julie was trapped somewhere. And if we freed her in time, we'd bring her back to life.

Emma was the missing puzzle piece that helped me to realize what had happened. And why Julie had killed herself. Julie had figured out that she'd have a second chance. And she knew I'd figure it out.

We split up. Gavin went hunting. He was going to hunt squads in the city and loot them. Dev got back in the Tesla and was going to look and ask around for a place we could find a guide to the dark place, to the center, to wherever the dead people go. It wouldn't be an easy task for Dev, but I knew he was up to it.

I was going to the dance floor, which was in the center of the city, on top of the tallest building in the city. I walked towards it, trying to act as if I were an NPC so that no squads tried to kill me.

Unfortunately, a squad did see me.

They started to shoot at me from across the street, but I hopped a fence into an alley and took off running. I made a couple random turns down alleys until I got away from the squad.

Then I made it to the skyscraper.

I went into the lobby, signed up for the breakdancing competition at the front desk, and went into the elevator. It took me up one hundred and twenty floors where there was a bouncer whose name was Jeff. He was fat, but amiable. He let me through the door which led to the open rooftop. But not before he explained that the dance floor was a gun-neutral zone. Our guns wouldn't work if we tried to use them out there. There was to be no fighting. Only dancing.

There were tons of people here, NPCs and real people, students who looked to be my age. At least a hundred competitors.

I knew I could do this. Gavin wasn't going to mess it up for me this time and I already had my routine worked out. I had to wait my turn though.

I asked some of the real students who were waiting their turns how they'd ended up on this island. They all said the same thing. They'd gotten detention. I also asked some of them if they knew anything about the underworld. None of them did. Half of them were wearing necklaces that were glowing blue. I guessed the other half had discarded theirs, even though the orientation video had told us not to.

Gavin was half-way up a building, peering out the window with a sniper rifle. Taking his time. He saw a squad of three guys. Must have lost one member. He lined up each shot. Killed all three. Headshots. Then he waited to make sure another squad wasn't going to show up. When they didn't, he ran down the stairs onto the street, looted the dead players. Got ten thousand credits.

Dev was hopping around taxis and trying to avoid squads. He had a squad on his tail—and they were driving a Camaro. Not as fast as the Tesla, though. Dev was reading all the street signs. Trying to find a place he could get some information. He was wracking his brain, trying to get an idea. All Allen had told him was to find a guide to the place where dead people go.

How did Allen even know there was such a place on Death Island?

How did he know there was still a chance for Julie and Emma?

Dev couldn't figure it out.

But he trusted his friend.

Speeding around a corner, he saw a large building fronted by tall marble columns. A Library. He knew he'd get information there.

Finally, it was my turn. I was doing this for Julie. I let go of all my anxiety and nervousness. I didn't have any fear or sweat. I was confident in myself, knew I could do this. My requested song started playing. I walked onto the dance floor, strides on point. Then I broke it down. I nailed my routine. Perfectly. After I finished, I had to sit around and wait for all the contestants to complete their routines.

Gavin saw two teammates driving down one of the streets in a taxi they'd quite obviously stolen from an NPC. He lifted his bazooka. Shot their car dead on. The entire car burst to pieces and he got two kills in one shot. He looted them for four hundred credits.

He realized people didn't carry a lot credits.

He hoped Allen won the dance battle and knew what he was talking about. Gavin had to admit, though he hated admitting it. Allen was a better leader than he. He would never admit it out loud though. Never. He still hated Allen.

He had his reasons.

But he would help.
For Julie.

4

Julie woke up feeling really hot. Before she even opened her eyes she realized she was drenched in sweat, all down her back, dripping down her face, soaked into her hair. Then her eyes snapped open and she looked around. It was bright here. Sitting up, she saw that she was laying a foot away from lava. She was on a rock—a really hot rock. There was a lake of lava before her, stretching as far as the eye could see.

She smiled, despite her terrible circumstances, because she realized that she'd been right. She knew that if she'd killed herself, she would still be alive somewhere else. She'd have a chance for survival. She wiped sweat from her forehead, feeling much better though she was burning up.

There was still a chance she would die, unless Allen figured out what she had.

She figured if Allen got Emma to The Professor and fixed the island, Julie would automatically come back to life.

It was easy enough to figure it all out. The team that had kidnapped her and was using her to try to get the location of The Professor had given it away. Basically, Liam's motivation was to kill The Professor so that a team couldn't save the island that way. He wanted to win the Battle Royale. He wanted the island to be destroyed and everything in it.

Julie had asked herself: *Why didn't Liam just kill Emma?*

If Liam were to kill Emma, it would effectively destroy the island. The Professor had said that he needed his daughter to save the island. Which meant that all Liam had to do was kill Emma to ruin everything. He didn't need to kill or capture The Professor.

But he did.

He needed him because he knew that even if he killed Emma she would still be alive somewhere else. Down here. In an underworld type of place. And as long as she was alive, teams would still be able to find her. He needed to get to The Professor and capture and hide him. Not kill him. Because if he knew about this underworld place, then other teams would know about it or figure it out.

Julie knew that it would be a challenge to escape from here.

It was most likely impossible for her to do it alone.

But if Allen put together the pieces, he would realize

there was an underworld somewhere. He would come for her later, after completing the mission of bringing Emma to The Professor.

Julie heard a noise to her right.

Looking over, her eyes opened wide. She felt like she'd been gut punched. She lost her breath for a moment. Because just to her right a girl was waking up—Emma.

Emma had been killed!

Which slightly ruined her plan.

"Emma," Julie said, moving over to her.

Emma was shaking her head, clearly in pain. She looked afraid. Really afraid. She hugged Julie, clinging to her. "Where are we?"

"In hell, basically."

"Are we dead?"

"Not yet."

"How do you know?"

"Allen will come for us."

"How do you know?"

Julie pictured Allen. For all of his cockiness, all of his pride and flaws, he was still the best guy she knew. She hadn't been lying to him when she'd told him she had feelings for him. She had. She'd been dating Gavin because Gavin was always around. He was her next-door neighbor. Their families were friends. Gavin's parents were rich like her parents and her parents encouraged the relationship. She was dating him just because.

Because she felt like she was supposed to.

She kind of liked him, in a way. He was strong and kind to her. He was popular and cool. He was a little smart. He had to get average grades to be on the football team. And they had lots of memories together.

Allen was a poor kid, from the other side of town. He didn't feel like he mattered. He compared himself to others too often. Julie wanted him to realize for himself that he was special before she dated him. But she did want to date him, even if her mom didn't approve. And her mom most definitely didn't approve.

Because her mom only saw money and not potential. Allen had more potential than any guy she'd ever known or would ever know. He was brimming with life and dreams and hopes and goals.

Would he reach all of them?

Probably not.

But she knew that if she was with him, she'd be his strength. That he'd find a path that brought him more truth and warmth than he could have planned for himself.

She knew this in her bones.

Somehow she knew.

"He'll come for us," said Julie.

Emma was crying.

"What's wrong?" Julie asked.

"I'm scared."

Julie noticed her necklace was still green. It was green because she'd activated her strength. It wasn't giving her any special power-ups or anything. Her theory was that if all of her teammates activated the adjectives on their necklaces, they would receive power-ups. As far as she knew, she was the only one whose necklace had been activated.

She'd done it by being strong.

She'd always known she was strong, but she didn't always use her strength because oftentimes people (like her mom) confused her strength with anger and impulsiveness. But Julie could tell the difference of when she was being angry rather than impulsive. And she oftentimes did give into anger. But not this time. Not on Death Island.

She was only going to be strong here.

Because she was.

Allen needed to learn that he was worthy and that he mattered in the grand scheme of things. That he actually was as special as he often dreamed and deep down knew he was. Gavin needed to learn to be humble and follow Allen's lead. And Dev needed to learn courage, because oftentimes he was afraid and stayed back when he should run forward.

Julie understood the island now.

She hoped it wasn't too late.

5

The Library had given Dev directions to a location a bit out of town where they could hire a guide. First, he needed to pickup his friends.

Dev found them at the breakdance competition. He walked onto the roof the moment they announced Allen was the winner. Dev knew Allen would win. That was a million credits, plus the bit of credits and loot Gavin had grinded out.

They took it to the store and Dev purchased the EMP even though Allen and Gavin objected. The EMP was a million credits, which only left them just enough for the guide (Dev had learned the price) and a few weapons.

They got one more health potion since Dev had used the one they had to heal Gavin.

Then they got into the Tesla and started heading out of town.

"You sure about the EMP?" asked Allen. "You think it will actually help?"

Dev winked at Allen.

He knew something Allen didn't know, or at least, wasn't thinking of.

"You sure about this guide?" Allen asked.

Dev nodded.

"You sure this will work to save Julie?" asked Gavin.

Julie was holding Emma's hand, running away from the lava. She'd found out that Emma was their age—fourteen. But Emma wasn't as strong, couldn't handle this experience as well as Julie. They were in a giant cave of sorts. It was bright because of the lava. But Julie was running towards the darkness, towards the unknown. She didn't have a flashlight or any equipment on her person. She'd lost her inventory when she'd died.

"That was brave what you did," said Emma, as they ran. "I wouldn't have been able to do it."

Julie took them into the darkness, where everything was dim and her eyes had to adjust. Then she found a cave within the cave. Decided to go into it. Because where else was there to go?

It was tight, a pathway of only a few feet wide.

It reminded her of being on Tom Sawyer's Island at Disney Land.

Then she saw a light in the ceiling. Crystals.

There were glowing crystals in the ceiling. They

showed the path forward. Which was good because one side of the pathway opened up and became a cliff. It dropped off into something that sounded like water far below. Julie stopped for a moment, squatted, and looked over the edge. She could make out a pool of water far below. It was glimmering under the glowing crystal light.

Then they continued.

"Where are we going?" asked Emma.

"We're going," said Julie, not really answering the question.

Julie obviously didn't have a plan.

She just hoped a plan would present itself.

We made it to the guide's house. It was a small shack of a house hidden on one side of a small hill. There was one tall tree standing over it on one side. We parked our Tesla beside the shack. I knocked on the door. No answer. I knocked on the door again. No answer.

"Hello!" I yelled. "We need your help!"

"Yo," a voice said from inside. "Come in."

I opened the door cautiously. The inside was lit by a combination of candles and lava lamps. The floor was dirt with a rug over it. The "guide" was sitting on the floor, playing an Xbox on a small monitor. He was playing *Fortnite* and wasn't looking up from the screen.

"Are you our guide?" I asked.

"Yeah. I'm Eli."

He was probably nineteen. He was focused on his game. Didn't even look up at us.

"Hold up, bros," he said. "Trying to get this dub."

"We don't have much time," I said.

Just then he fell off a mountain and died.

He threw off his headset and threw his controller aside. "That game sucks," he said. "I hate it but I play it all the time." Then he looked up at me. "Hey, you want to buy my Xbox One? It's in good condition. I'll give it to you for three hundred cash. Right now. Have a deal?" He extended his hand for a shake.

"Ummm… I'm here to hire you. I don't want your Xbox, no."

"Aigth, aight. What can I help you with?"

"We need to go to the underworld, wherever that is."

"We call it the CENTER," he said.

"Take us there," I said.

"That will be ten thousand credits," he said.

Gavin paid him.

"All right boys! Let's go."

And he walked out the door.

Then he walked back in. "Oh, let's get some supplies first."

He was kind of a strange guide, but whatever. I'm glad we'd found one.

There was an opening at the end of this tunnel. Plenty of light was coming through. There was a wooden sign at the top of the exit that read, "EXIT THE CENTER. THIS WAY." — And it had an arrow indicating they were on the right path. The arrow was pointed up. Stepping through the tunnel, Julie was floored by what she saw.

It was the Earth during the Jurassic era. She knew this because there was molten lava in different corners and running through ravines. The Earth was mostly rock with some overgrown weeds covering swaths of areas. And there were dinosaurs everywhere. Some were warring with each other. Some were running in packs. The sun was out and blazing down on them.

"Are we back on Death Island?" Emma asked.

"Not even close," said Julie. "Somehow we have to get out of here."

Julie looked to the sky. There were pterodactyls soaring overhead. She watched them for a few moments, considering how the hell they were supposed to escape from this hell. Pun intended.

Then she realized the giant dinosaur birds were coming towards them.

She'd seen those birds in movies, had read about them, and knew they were killers.

Emma squeezed Julie's shoulder, pointing.

Julie looked over and saw a safari type of jeep just a hundred yards from them. Just sitting there. It looked to be in perfect condition. She hoped the keys were in it because she started sprinting for it, dragging Emma behind her. The sun was so hot she was already sweating.

Now she knew how the dinosaurs had gone extinct.

From the sun.

The birds were roaring in the sky—what sounded like high screeches. They sounded angry, though Julie realized they had no reason to be angry. They were probably just hungry.

That's when she realized the jeep was right on the edge of a cliff. And the ground underneath the jeep was starting to break. If it did break, the jeep would fall deep into a ravine of lava.

She let go of Emma's hand because the girl was slowing her down.

Sprinted for the jeep!

6

Eli climbed into the backseat of the Tesla with them and had them put the coordinates to The Center in the Tesla's navigational system.

Gavin was sitting beside him in the back seat. "Are you sure you're qualified for this job?" Gavin asked. "You've had sufficient training?"

Eli looked dazed, didn't answer for a few moments. Then, at length, he said, "It's no sweat, broskies."

"I am not sure about this guy," said Gavin.

"He's our only shot," I said.

"Which is usually why people hire me," said Eli.

"Are you the only guide?" Dev asked.

"No. But I'm the cheapest, and the nearest to the city. Freakin' Ralph has had more successful missions than I have. And Troy and Angel and Aaron and Zack and Evan."

"How many successful missions have you led?"

"This will be my first," said Eli.

"But we haven't started the mission yet," Gavin said.

"We got this, boys," said Eli. "Don't sweat it."

"I wish you'd stop saying that," said Gavin.

Dev kept the pedal to the metal. We were flying over hills, through the fields, at over a hundred MPH the entire time. I think we might have accidentally run over a few bunnies.

FINALLY, after what felt like forever, we reached the base of a giant mountain. It was the tallest mountain I'd seen in my life.

"Go up," said Eli. "One must go up before they go down."

Then Eli laughed to himself.

Gavin punched him in the shoulder, which made him stop laughing.

"Up the mountain," he said, extending his long arm. He was really tall and had really long arms. Didn't look like a mountain-man guide.

Dev started up the mountain.

It was going to be a deadly climb. It was dangerously steep, dotted with rock outcroppings, large bushes, divots, all kinds of stuff.

"What's the best path?" Dev asked.

Eli shrugged. "Just don't crash."

It would have been easier if we all had individual dirt

bikes. Or a jeep. Or something meant for driving up mountains. Luckily the Tesla could jump.

Julie jumped into the driver's seat of the jeep. Emma was far behind. The ground beneath the jeep cracked away more from the mainland. She dropped a foot, and the jeep started sliding to the right, towards the cliff. Julie looked around for the keys. Checked the dashboard and the center console and the overhead thing. Then she saw that they were already in ignition. She twisted them. The jeep hummed to life. She jammed her foot on the gas and shot away from the sloped floor just as it fell away into the lava with a giant splash. The birds were swooping down towards Emma, but Julie scared them away by doing a spinning donut around Emma. They flew upwards, to circle—to come back in for the kill. Julie screeched to a halt for Emma to climb in.

Once Emma was seat belted in, Julie said, "Hold on."

Then she took off towards the larger dinosaurs, to cross the old land.

Sweat was dripping down her face, soaked in her hair. Sun was beating down through the sunroof of the jeep. The jeep was fast. They were crossing territory fast. But the valley extended out as far as the eye could see. A herd of nice looking dinosaurs showed up on their right side, running beside them. Keeping up with the jeep at seventy miles per hour.

Emma started to scream.

"They're nice," said Julie.

The jeep didn't have doors, so one felt exposed sitting in the seats, like the dinosaurs could easily get to them.

Just then, one of the "nice" dinosaurs rammed the jeep,

nearly hitting Emma. It rammed it so hard that the jeep moved over a foot on the rock. The tires screeched.

Julie started going faster, though it felt dangerous because they were bouncing over the uneven land. Going ninety MPH they pulled away from the herd.

But just ahead were two T-Rex's going at each other, either playing or fighting. Julie couldn't tell which. She hoped they wouldn't see her.

But they did. They heard the engine, stopped fighting, and looked at the jeep as she went towards them. Julie couldn't go to the right because there was a lava ravine and she wanted to stay as far away from that as she could. She couldn't go to the left because there was a large stand of trees and she didn't want to waste time going all the way around it. Plus, she didn't know what was on the far side of it. There could be worse things on that side.

So she had to try to dodge the t-rex's.

She pushed the jeep up to one hundred MPH.

Dev took them around a rock outcropping, but then the mountain got so steep and there didn't seem to be any place for us to go. We'd been at this for the last fifteen minutes. I was tense in my seat, hoping we'd make it. Trying to will us up the mountain. My seatbelt was locked because the car was so vertically inclined.

Dev tried taking us up and over a large rock, but the tires started slipping out. Then they caught and we shot forward and upward. But there was a tree directly before us. Dev swerved to the right, taking us onto another rock. We went sharply to the right. Problem was, just a few feet under our car the mountain dropped off for a least a hundred yard fall. That's the size of a football field. The tires were slipping out. Not catching. We were only a few feet from the cliff. Dev was trying to drive us away from it to no avail. The tires were screeching, burning rubber, creating smoke. Slowly but surely we were falling closer and closer to the edge of the cliff.

"You know Teslas can fly, right?" said Eli calmly.

"You're messing?!" said Dev, sounding angry.

"Am not," said Eli, reaching over the center console and pressing a button that had a logo with a pair of wings on it on the dash. Suddenly, the Tesla lifted off the rock, into the air, floating. Dev still had his foot on the pedal so we shot upwards. Flying! *We were actually flying!*

"You couldn't have said that earlier, Eli!" I yelled. "That would have been helpful when we were at the base of the mountain."

"I forgot," said Eli.

"How could you have forgotten?" I said.

Dev was yelling at him too.

"What is wrong with you, lanky man?" said Gavin.

Then Gavin punched him in the shoulder again.

Eli whined. "Jeez. Take it easy. We all make mistakes."

We flew fast to the top of the mountain. Dev spiraled us to the top, then leveled us out at the top. We realized once we were at the top that this was no ordinary mountain. It was a volcano. There was no lava that we could see but there was a big hole in the top.

"Let me guess," I said. "We're jumping down?"

"Presto," said Eli.

"What are you?!" asked Dev. "Some kind of magic man."

"10-4," said Eli.

The opening was wide, definitely large enough for a car.

Without hesitating, Dev plunged us down into the hole. He turned the brights on, shining the car's headlights deep. We could see nothing but the sides of the tunnel as we sped down it. Into darkness.

Suddenly it started to smell really bad. Which was weird because all the windows were up.

"What is that awful smell?" asked Gavin. "It smells like a skunk died."

"Sorry guys," said Eli. "I farted."

"Gross," I said.

"And I took off my shoes and my feet stink," Eli said. "Really badly, actually."

"Freakin' put your shoes back on, man!" said Gavin.

"You right. You right," he said.

"Why would you take them off in the first place?" asked Gavin, very angry.

Eli put up his hands, scared. "Don't punch me!"

Dev rolled down the windows. The air was warm down here. Felt nice, actually. I wasn't scared for myself. Or us. Only for Julie. This was our only chance to save her.

7

Julie went literally between the legs of one of the t-rex. Then they raced past a pit full of raptors that were fighting each other, like some kind of UFC competition. Then they went off a small jump. The jeep landed on the rocky surface, bouncing a little. Julie almost lost control.

She continued speeding across the land, dodging dinosaurs and lava pits and large rocks and skeletons of dinosaurs, until finally she slammed on the brakes and the jeep slid to a stop because she saw something even crazier than a jeep. She saw an airplane—the old-fashioned kind. A small propeller plane with only two seats. They only needed two seats.

She drove the jeep to it.

"We're switching vehicles," Julie said.

"You know how to fly?" asked Emma.

Julie didn't answer. She didn't know how but she was sure she would figure it out. They jumped into the plane. There were long-necked calm dinosaurs nearby, chewing on the tall trees.

It didn't take Julie long to figure it out.

She got the plane going, then took off down a stretch of land. With a minute, they were airborne, flying over the land. Julie felt much safer in the air. For a few seconds. Her heart rate took off the moment she saw them—the pterodactyls. Four of them this time, flying towards them, backlit by the bright sun swooping in for the kill. Each of the birds was bigger than the plane.

They could easily take the plane down.

And this was their only chance out of this place.

Julie took them higher into the sky. The propellers were working hard. The pterodactyls were faster and could change direction easier. They were coming in fast.

"Hold on!" Julie yelled.

We reached the bottom of the volcano tunnel. Dev piloted us into a giant cavern that glowed red. Rocks were floating on the inside of it, kind of like asteroids. He dodged them as he flew us through.

"Where do we go?" asked Dev.

"I don't know. Never made it this far," said Eli, eating a candy bar. "Hey, anyone want the rest of this? I can't finish it. I'm so full. I had a freakin' turkey leg earlier today. It was bomb."

"Focus up, man!" said Gavin. "We need to get to the

Center."

"I'm sure we're almost there."

"How can you be sure?"

"I'm actually not sure."

We realized now that Eli would be no help. We continued through the cavern. Exiting it, we found ourselves in another world entirely. A hot world. I saw lava spew up just in front of us, from a hole in the ground. Dev swerved around it. There was a lake of water ahead. There was a sun over our heads—a really hot one.

There were palm trees all around the lake. I saw a monster pop his head out of the lake—a prehistoric, ancient looking monster. Then it ducked back under. That's when I realized that the moving creatures in the distance were dinosaurs. They were far away.

Since our windows were rolled down, I heard a faint noise. Far ahead I saw a few dots moving around in the sky. As we neared and Dev got us going faster, I realized that one of the dots was a propeller plane. Flying around. I wondered if it was Julie.

"Go towards them," I said.

Dev sped us up.

8

Julie dodged the four predators by swerving beneath them at the last moment. But they were turned around, flapping their wings, coming in fast.

This old plane wouldn't be fast enough to get away.

So she headed for the lake.

They would need to crash land.

She saw something flying over the lake—probably another bird. Which sucked. But she kept going. Glancing back, she saw the four giant dinosaur birds just behind her.

She lowered the plane. Fast.

The lake was large and had waves, which was weird

because what was causing the waves? She didn't know. It was surrounded by a strip of beach and palm trees. Mountains rose up at the end of a long valley on one side. There were plenty of dinosaurs on the land far below them.

Then one of the birds broke off the tail of the plane.

The plane started spinning in circles, uncontrollably.

She tried to correct it as best as she could.

After a minute of fighting it, she got them leveled out and flying straight. The propellers were glitching out. And finally the propellers stopped going. Now they were gliding.

One of the birds flew just overhead, barely missing Julie and Emma's heads.

The lake was still too far away. They were going to crash land on the rocks and surely die.

"The plane is broken," said Dev. "I can't hear it anymore."

"It's getting swarmed by those giant birds," I said.

"Pterodactyls."

"Crazy," I said.

"Oh, yeah, did I forget to mention this place is filled with dinosaurs?" Eli said.

We weren't paying attention to him anymore.

He was the most worthless guide ever.

"Go faster," I said.

"We're at max speed," he said.

We were at least a minute out from the plane, and the plane was falling fast, about to crash land. If Julie was in it, she would die surely. And I knew that if you die in here, you're dead for sure. There are no more resets. No more underworlds. This was Julie's last chance.

Julie tried to pull up on the control yoke, tried to keep the plane flying, but it was going down faster than fast. "Hold on, Emma!" she shouted. Not that holding on would help them any.

A pterodactyl flew fast towards the Tesla. Gavin climbed out the window and onto the roof of the Tesla, started taking shots at the bird and shot it out of the sky.

I hoped against hope we'd reach the plane in time.

We were closing in fast.

Then we got close enough that I could see Julie's blue hair. And there was a girl in the seat behind her—Emma! They were both here. They'd been taken down by the birds, which were still circling the plane. Gavin was taking shots at the birds. I saw one of the four go down in a spray of blood.

"Great job!" I yelled. "Now bring us close," I said to Dev.

"How are we going to catch them?"

I turned back to Eli. He was playing with the rope around his belt, tying different kinds of knots with them. "This knot looks like a bunny," he said.

I grabbed the rope from out of his hands.

"Hey!" he said.

I started tying it around one of my feet. I was going to jump from the car, hang down, and catch Julie and Emma out of the plane. It wouldn't be easy. I wasn't even sure if it was possible, but it was my only idea because I could clearly see that they weren't going to make it all the way to the lake. They were going to land down on the rock and die—probably in a fiery explosion.

"That's crazy," said Dev, noticing my plan.

"I'll help," said Eli.

I had no idea what he was talking about.

When we had almost reached the girls, Eli opened his door and jumped out. Without a rope! At first I thought maybe he knew something we didn't. Like, maybe he could fly or something. Or maybe he had a parachute. He didn't. I heard him yelling *tally-ho!* And then he landed flat on the floor far below like a pancake. He died. And that was the last we saw of Eli.

I tied the other end of the rope around the passenger seat.

Then, when we were almost there, I lowered myself out of the Tesla. The rope extended twenty-five feet down. Gavin was looking over at me from the roof. "Be careful!" he yelled.

I was being careful.

The rope went tight and I was hanging down, arms reaching.

"Lower!" I yelled to Dev.

The plane was just ahead, coming in hot. Smoke was trailing out the back. A pterodactyl flew just over my head, trying to swipe at the rope. It hit it! It didn't break, but it swung me way out of the way and caused me to start spinning in circles. I couldn't see and was suddenly super dizzy. I already had a problem with dizziness to begin with. I sometimes get dizzy when I'm just standing around. Spinning was the worst thing for me. I felt like clothes in a dryer. I tried to stop the spinning, figure out a way to slow it down. I started doing sort-of half crunches in the air. To get steady.

"Almost there," I heard Dev yelling.

"Allen!" I heard Julie yell. But I couldn't see her. I was still spinning and everything was a blur. I was also swinging as if I were a pendulum in a grandfather clock. Long swings. There was no way I could catch both girls swinging like this.

As we got even closer, it slowed down and I got control.

We were only about twenty feet from the girls and they were coming in fast.

I looked up and saw Dev had his head out the window, looking, trying to judge the distances. Gavin was up there as well, looking over from the roof of the car, yelling instructions at Dev. Then a pterodactyl nearly took Gavin off the roof of the car, but Gavin was quick to shoot him.

Now there were two pterodactyls.

I wasn't sure if I could catch the girls, though!

9

I reached out my hands. It was all up to Dev at this point. He brought me to them, then he turned the Tesla around to track with the plane. We were flying down with the plane. The ground was looming large, only a few football fields away. We had only seconds before we'd crash land. Arms dangling down, the fingertips on my right hand began to brush Emma's.

So close!

So freakin' close!

I was straining and reaching as best I could.

"Lower!" I shouted with all my might.

Just then, Dev dropped me low enough that I could

reach both of their hands. I grabbed both hands, holding them as tightly as I could. Then Dev pulled away. Almost too hard. I almost lost grip of Julie's hand. Luckily they'd unbuckled from the plane, and they slid right out of their seats.

Dev pulled up and piloted us towards the lake.

The plane crashed below us seconds later on the rocky ground in a fiery explosion. Bits of metal flew skyward, nearly hitting us. That's when the pterodactyl hit our rope once more. Except this time I was holding the weight of two girls. I wasn't as strong as Gavin. I could barely keep my grip. But I was determined to keep it. We were spinning and swinging once more and my stomach wanted to puke. It was worse than the spinning plate ride Petrov had put in at our school—and that ride always made me throw up. I was trying to hold in my puke right now.

Dev was going to drop us off in the lake because there was no way of pulling us into the car. There was some danger in the lake because I had seen a monster in it. I hoped that wherever we landed the monster would be nowhere near us.

I heard gunshots going off overhead as Gavin tried to pick off the birds for us so that we didn't have to worry about them. Next thing I knew I felt the rope go loose!

At first I thought the pterodactyls had cut us loose.

I thought we were going to die.

We were all screaming.

But then we crash landed into the water! Giant waves went up around us because we'd fallen a good fifty feet. All my body ached from hitting the water in a weird way, like, almost a belly flop. Dev had cut us loose.

Since we'd fallen so far, we sunk far.

I opened my eyes under the water. It was bright enough, and I saw that Julie and Emma were swimming for the surface. I was glad Emma could swim. One less thing to worry about.

Then I was clambering for the surface alongside them.

I couldn't see the monster anywhere.

But that didn't mean that he wasn't near.

Turns out he was—because I heard a loud underwater growl coming from beneath us, from the darkness below.

10

Swimming fast, we made it to the surface of the water. Without getting eaten. Which was surprising. The Tesla was lowering down to the water. Dev was being careful not to accidentally come in too fast and submerge the vehicle, which would probably break it. Unless it was waterproof. But there was no way to know whether or not it was.

He was going so slow.

Gavin was still shooting at the final remaining pterodactyl.

"Faster!" I yelled to Dev.

We were treading water.

The beast beneath us roared once more.

Finally, Dev lowered so that the tires of the car were touching the top of the water. I let Julie climb in first. Then I climbed in and reached back down for Emma's hand. I got her hand and pulled her into the backseats.

"Go!" I yelled to Dev.

But he didn't go.

I looked to him. He was pressing buttons on the dashboard, frantic.

"Go!" I yelled again.

"Something's wrong!" he yelled back.

I could see a status bar on the screen on the dash. It was maxed out. And a warning signal read, OVERHEATED.

"What does that mean?" I asked.

Before Dev could answer, the Tesla engine shut off and we fell into the water. For the first few seconds the Tesla was floating, which I thought was weird. But then we started sinking, fast. All the windows were open and the inside began to fill up with water.

Dev was turning the car on and off, flipping switches and knobs, kicking the gas pedal down. The water was up to our knees. Then to our thighs. The water came up over the seats.

"Hold on," said Dev.

"To what?!" said Julie. "We're going to drown in here."

Gavin was still on the roof. "Guys!" he was yelling. "What's going on in there?"

I was pretty afraid. The car was getting drenched—the inside and the engine. I was afraid it wouldn't turn back on. I didn't know much about cars or Teslas. I most certainly didn't know they could fly. But I knew this couldn't be good.

"Dev," I said, flatly. "Dev!" I yelled.

"Working on it!" he yelled.

As if in response to his yelling, the beast in the water roared beneath us. Then struck the bottom of the car, pushing us up two feet. Then it left and we started dropping once more.

"There's something in the water," Gavin yelled.

"No duh!" I yelled back.

Then Gavin started shooting into the water. I hoped he wasn't just blindly shooting, that he was actually aiming for the monster. But I guess anything helped.

That's when the engine sputtered to life.

We all smiled and made happy noises.

The engine died.

We all made sad noises. Our smiles became frowns.

Then the engine came to life once more. Louder, this time.

We didn't make noises this time. We were too tense, too afraid to get let down. I saw the monster's head pop out just in front of us, its giant mouth open and ready to take a bite out of our poor and magnificent Tesla. But before it could, Dev lifted us out of the water and shot us towards the sky. The bar on the visual display was still dangerously close to the red, about to overheat once more.

"Slow down, buddy," I said.

He did.

Problem was, the final pterodactyl was coming at us from the side. Gavin was unloading his rifle at it but missing all the shots. In his defense, the bird was dodging every direction—was not an easy target. That's when the volcano started rumbling. The entire ground started vibrating. Then, within a few seconds, it was completely shaking side to side. It was a surreal sight.

I watched through my window as the palm trees around the lake swayed side to side violently as if getting pummeled by the strongest wind ever. Except that there was no wind. It was a giant earthquake—the tectonic plates shifting violently and shaking the trees. Dev was piloting us back towards the red cave—towards the exit. The entrance to the cave was shifting side to side.

"We're not going to make it!" yelled Julie.

Dev floored the Tesla, but the red bar rose significantly.

The engine started to sputter.

He lowered our speed.

We couldn't go top speed. We'd been pushing the car to extremes for the entire time we'd had it. Turns out, you have to treat cars nicely.

On the bright side, Gavin shot down the last pterodactyl.

Then we plummeted into the cave.

Asteroids were floating all around within the cave. Dev had a harder time dodging them because he had to go much slower and because they were bouncing around more violently what with the shaking of the core of the Earth.

Gavin climbed back into the backseats.

"We need speed," he said.

We all nervously laughed.

"We don't have that option," Dev said calmly.

Then we were back in the giant tunnel from which we'd descended to get into this place. I saw the lava, just five feet under us, bubbling, ready to burst. It hadn't been there before.

Dev aimed us upwards.

Apparently flying straight up took a toll on the engine. The meter that indicated the engine's core temperature turned red once more.

I had my fingers crossed, and I was pressed back against my seat from gravity.

On the other bright side, we'd rescued Julie and Emma. Emma was in the seat between Gavin and I.

"Hi again," I said. "Glad to find you."

"Glad to be found," she said.

"How are you doing, Julie?" I asked.

"Just fine, thank you!" she shouted angrily.

"I figured it out!"

"I'm glad!" she yelled, angrily, obviously nervous about this escape route.

That's when the lava below decided to burst upwards, towards us, coming in hot (pun intended).

"Dev," I said calmly. "Must go faster."

"I know, buddy," he said. "Great *Jurassic Park* reference, btw."

"You like it?"

"Always love a *Jurassic Park* reference," he said.

"We should watch it after we get off Death Island. Like, a movie night."

"Guys!" Julie yelled.

"What?" said Dev calmly.

"Shut the freak up!"

"Okay!" said Dev. "But for sure on the movie night."

We were all laughing now. Not because we thought we were being funny. Because we were terrified. Gavin, Emma and I were turned back, looking out the back window, watching the lava coming dangerously close.

Within three feet. Then within one foot.

Dev stepped on the pedal a bit more.

We pulled away by a foot, but then the lava started exploding and rising even faster. It started to touch the back end of the car.

I looked forward, watching the meter.

It was one percentile away from overheating.

If it were to overheat, the car would shut off and we'd be consumed by the lava. We'd die instantly, with no recourse. With no way to escape THE CENTER. With no hope to win. With no hope to get off the island.

It was all or nothing.

Showdown At Pacific Peaks

1

We crash landed outside the volcano, on the side of the
mountain. We'd made it out alive! The Tesla had got
burned up and was starting to catch on fire. We landed in
tall grass and jumped out of the car in case it exploded.
We started running down the hill because lava was spilling
out the top of the mountain. There were no vehicles
anywhere that we could see.

We were in a wide valley. The valley rose to a hill, and
we couldn't see what was over it. We ran for it
nonetheless.

Two things.

One, I was incredibly grateful we'd escaped and had

gotten Julie and Emma out alive.

Two, Dev's necklace was glowing green. He'd found his courage. He had surely been courageous, piloting us out of the volcano. Gavin's and my necklaces were the only ones still blue. We made it to the top of the hill and saw a stand that was selling lemonade and dirt bikes for credits. Emma apparently had fifty thousand credits. We spent twenty of the thousand on two ATVs and a dirt bike. The dirt bike was for me. Gavin and Emma took one of the ATVs. I told Gavin to take Emma because he would be the best at keeping her safe. Surprisingly, he listened and agreed. Dev and Julie took the other. Dev drove—he'd already proved to be a great driver.

And of course we all downed a glass of lemonade.

Then we started tearing up dirt across the valley as the sun started to rise on the horizon. Dev had purchased a map from the city and, as such, was leading us to Pacific Peaks.

To The Professor.

To win the game.

2

We made it to Pacific Peaks.

It had taken hours.

It was beautiful, especially in the early morning sun. We were hidden behind a rock outcropping, a safe distance away. I was looking through binoculars. Pacific Peaks was basically a giant beach. It wasn't a typical beach, however, in that the sea spread out around a lot of small mountains and peaks. The tops of the mountains were covered in snow. The base of the mountains were beautiful looking beaches. The place was very bright and colorful, with lots of inlets and lagoons.

And squads.

The sea had flooded most of the island, and the tidal waves were sounding off more than ever. Everyone was pressed into this last location. There were hundreds of remaining players. We could see a bunch of them fighting on jet skis and boats—some of the boats were on the water but most of the jet skis and boats had the capability of flying. They were flying between the mountains, soaring over the water, and the squads were shooting each other out of the sky. Some were up in the snowy parts of the mountains, fighting. Some were rappelling down the mountain. Some were trying to climb. It was a war zone.

I looked to the tallest mountain. A few of the mountains were so tall that they went up past the clouds. There was one in particular that I could tell was the tallest. It went way up past the clouds. That's where The Professor would be. At the very top.

We would never make it with our dirt bikes.

It would take too long to climb.

But everyone was getting their boats and jet skis from somewhere. I scanned the beach until I found a rental shack. We'd have to stop there and blow the rest of our credits. Then we'd have to get Emma to the top of the main mountain. I was afraid that the moment we stepped out from this outcropping we'd get sniped. There were so many teams all around.

I wondered if Liam and his squad were here. I hoped he hadn't learned of The Professor's location from another team. There was only one way to find out. We ran out from the outcropping, towards the rental place.

3

Liam was flying around Pacific Peaks, owning people.

He loved how good he was at Battle Royale.

He loved that he was wreaking havoc and killing off most of the teams single-handedly, getting lots of kills. Sure, technically he was cheating. He'd gotten special wristbands modified, which was against the rules of the island. There were similar to modded controllers. They allowed him to cheat. He was able to fly. He was able to turn invisible. And he was able to turn invincible and ultra-powerful for certain durations of time. He also had unlimited ammo. He was able to build forcefields around himself at any given time.

And he was crushing the competition.

Two of his squad members were still alive.

They weren't modded, but they had racked up enough credits to get jet skis that could fly. They flew behind him as he smashed through players. They were working their way to the top of the mountain.

Liam was pwning people.

Easily.

He would throw up a shield to block their bullets. Then fly towards them, turn himself invisible, then fly straight at them and shoot them or pound them off their vehicles so that they would fall to their death.

He knew The Professor was at the top of the mountain and he was determined to get there first. They were half-way up. He would kill The Professor. Then win the Battle Royale. His teacher had said that if they were to win this they would win a big prize.

He didn't care.

He just wanted to be known as the best. He was the best *Fortnite* streamer in the world. He loved being the best, being famous. This would make him even more famous. He would conquer Death Island. He would post it all over social media.

No one would be able to stop him.

4

I was trying to barter with the rental guy. He was an NPC and was therefore difficult to negotiate with. He wouldn't budge on the price. We could afford one flying boat—which could fit all of us. And one flying jet ski—which could fit one or two of us. I wanted to get jet skis for everyone. It seemed safer to fly apart. But it was all we could afford.

I transferred over the rest of our credits.

I let Gavin have the jet ski.

I went in the boat, let Dev pilot it.

I stood next to Emma, weapon at the ready, as Dev launched us towards the beaches. We soared fast towards the chaos, swerved around a corner of the base of one of the mountains into a gap between two mountains. Then pulled upwards to start flying up the side. Gavin was flying in front of us. His jet ski was equipped with a weapon that could fire straight ahead. There were some teams above us. He shot at an overhead boat, cutting it in half. The boat and the team started falling towards us. We dodged the wreckage and continued upward.

There were giant waterfalls falling on either side of us.

There was even one ravine that was flowing UP the mountain on one side of us. I told Dev to put our boat into it to see if it would make us faster. It did. We started traveling up the side, passing up Gavin. I shot a few players who were trying to scale the side of the mountain.

Then we randomly got sucked through the waterfall and into a secret entrance—like a tunnel within the mountain. We continued forward through the tunnel. There was no one in it that we could see. It was a shortcut! I saw the opening at the far end. We sped through it at top speed, Gavin behind us.

We all started yelling, our voices echoing.

It was awesome.

We shot out the opposite end of the tunnel, back into the sky. A boat was coming directly at us from the right. Dev pulled up and away. I started firing at them. They spun around to come at us. Too bad for them they didn't see Gavin. He didn't shoot them. He rammed his jet ski through their side. His jet ski was tipped with steel. Their boat got torn to bits and they all fell out of the sky.

We continued upward.

That's when I saw Liam.

Flying!

He was about two hundred feet from us, punching someone's boat in half. How was that even possible?

"He's cheating! Hacking!" said Dev.

I hated hackers. They were the worst. I didn't even play video games, but people who had to cheat at video games were the worst of the worst.

Dev tossed me his backpack.

"Why?" I asked.

"Just put it on. It has the EMP. In case we need it."

"You hold onto it," I said.

"No," he said. "You're going to need it. I have a bad feeling about this."

5

We still had a long way to go to get to the top of the peak. We weren't even close to the clouds and the mountain clearly extended higher than the clouds.

Dev was piloting us close to the mountain, within twenty feet.

Liam saw us.

I clearly saw him turn towards us, offer a half-smile, and float there for a few moments. His smile grew wider. I recognized people from his team behind him, on jet skis, shooting people out of the sky.

Dev gave the boat more throttle.

We started flying faster.

But not fast enough.

Liam flew directly towards us, FAST. He was coming in at the speed of a bullet. There was nothing we could do. There was nothing Dev could have done. Dev moved us really close to the mountain at the last moment. Which was the best thing he could have done.

Because Liam smashed through the direct center of our boat, breaking it into pieces. Emma had been the closest to me when it happened, so I grabbed her hand and leapt towards the side of the mountain. I didn't look before I'd leapt, but I'd had no choice. Facing the mountain in midair as the boat fell away from us, I landed on a tiny cleft on the side of the mountain. I grabbed onto a handhold in the rock, and kept my grip on Emma's hand strong. I swung her onto the cleft beside me. Turning around to see what had happened to my team, I saw them falling out of the sky.

They'd gotten knocked away from the mountain.

Julie and Dev were screaming as they fell away, and there was nothing I could do. Gavin, on the jet ski, had seen the whole thing. He piloted downwards, spiraling after our friends.

But before he could reach them, Liam flew down to them. He was holding a laser pistol in each hand. I saw the green bullets come from the guns as he executed Julie and Dev in midair.

Gavin pulled up and away.

Didn't even try to kill Liam or smash through him with the jet ski.

He was riding up towards me now.

"Noooooooo!" I yelled.

Not at Gavin. At the situation in particular.

I couldn't believe Julie had died again.

There was no possible way we could get back into the volcano because it had been flooded with lava. Adrenaline was coursing through my veins. For one moment, I felt like giving up. But only for a moment. Not even a moment. Half a moment. Because in the next moment I was totally and completely committed to completing the plan.

I had to get Emma to The Professor.

There was a chance that in doing so I could still save the world and bring Julie and Dev back. It had to work that way. In my bones, I knew it.

Sure. I wasn't sure.

But it was time to follow my instincts.

Gavin pulled up in the air beside me.

"Switch with me!" he yelled. "You and Emma will fit."

He jumped off the boat onto the cleft.

I noticed his blue necklace turned to green in that moment. And I realized why—because as I jumped through the small one foot gap onto the jet ski, Gavin explained. "You're more skilled than I am, Allen. I've always been jealous. That's why I've picked on you."

Emma climbed onto the back. Wrapped her arms around my waist.

Gavin and I really didn't have time to chat.

"You got this, bro," Gavin said.

I winked to him.

Just like that, we were friends.

Then I took off into the sky.

Looking downwards as I shot straight upwards towards the clouds I saw Gavin get hit full on by a rocket launcher. I looked away—I didn't want to see the blood and gore.

I kept my eyes forward. But Liam was capable of flying fast. I wasn't sure if we'd make it to the top. Not if he came after us. After a few seconds, I braved looking down. Liam was just a few football fields away. And he started flying towards us.

6

Gavin's necklace had turned green before he died. Which meant that everyone in my team had learned their lessons. Except for me apparently.

Worthiness. What did that even mean?

It meant, like, I was important or something.

I didn't feel very important. I just felt like I needed to get Emma to The Professor so that we could save this island. I felt scared. My heart was beating like crazy in my chest. And I felt that if I could get my necklace to turn green—since the rest of my team's were green—that I would get some kind of power-up. After all, the necklaces were apparently THE KEY.

Or something.

"I believe," I said under my breath.

Not even I could hear my own voice because the wind passing us and the sounds of the fighting going on all around.

"I believe," I said louder, barely hearing myself.

It was kind of embarrassing to say out loud, especially with Emma behind me. I said it once more. Then I decided, *What the heck?! I'm just gonna go for it.*

"I believe in myself!" I yelled.

I looked down at my necklace.

Nothing changed.

I didn't have many weapons. I didn't think Emma had any. She wasn't a fighting NPC. She was just someone I was supposed to save. Supposed to deliver to her father.

I had a pistol. A rifle across my back.

I had the EMP in the backpack.

I had a knife, from the mansion.

That was it.

In only a few seconds, Liam was catching up to us, about a hundred yards. We were shooting straight up. I started looking around the dashboard of the jet ski to find a way to make us go faster. Needed speed. More and more speed. Like a TURBO MODE or something.

Something else dawned on me.

If Liam wanted to torture me, he didn't need to kill me. He could simply pass me up, fly past me, through the clouds, to the top of the peak, and kill The Professor. If he killed either The Professor or Emma, there would be no more time to launch another rescue mission to the underworld.

He could easily pass me up and get to The Professor first and ruin everything.

I saw a jet ski come around the corner of the mountain. A guy with a sun-bleached tan, blonde, wearing a tank top and board shorts, was coming at us. He raised his pistol to shoot us. I noticed red in his eyes—an evil NPC lifeguard. He was dressed like a lifeguard from the beach—wearing red pants and a white shirt and a whistle around his neck.

Great.

More problems.

He took a few shots, but apparently missed all of them.

We continued skyward.

I looked down to see Liam bat the lifeguard out of the way, which slowed Liam down a second or two. Which was good for us. I would take all the advantage we could get.

I kept our nose pointed directly upward. We were riding alongside the edge of the mountain, maybe ten feet away. Flying fast!

I took a moment, but only a moment, to take it all in. We were on Death Island, having been flown out here by our billionaire school principal, and we were fighting in a real life Battle Royale. It was pretty insane. More than that, I was currently riding a jet ski that could fly.

Forget about aliens.

This was bigger than that.

This was actually happening.

Then my mind drifted elsewhere.

I saw my dad screaming at me so loud that I had to lock myself in the bathroom. He was in a drunken rage, pounding on the bathroom door, threatening to beat me up because I'd left a few dishes on the kitchen counter. "You worthless, worthless, no good, punk!" he screamed through the door, trying to break through it with his fists. "You're never going to be ANYTHING, Allen!"

He said those kinds of things to me often.

My mind flew through the memories.

But here I was, on this island, the only one with the blue necklace. I needed to figure out how to turn it green. I was trying to believe in myself but my dad's words were slamming through my mind. Like a stream. I blinked, trying to get them out of mind.

Then I heard Liam laughing behind us, which snapped me out of my daydreaming. I looked back and saw that he was probably only twenty-five yards away. Laughing and aiming his twin laser pistols. He started firing them at us. One after the other. I started spiraling our ship. The lasers past us on either side, flying by with fierce velocity and shooting up through the clouds.

Liam was gaining fast.

Shooting.

Laughing.

I took out my pistol, keeping one hand on the steering column. I aimed backwards, past Emma, and started shooting at Liam. My fourth shot hit his arm. He yelped in pain, then was growling, essentially, more angry than ever. Coming at us faster than ever.

We were almost to the clouds.

"We need speed!" Emma yelled.

I started laughing with nervousness, at the craziness of the situation. Like, no duh. We needed speed. We needed our team. We needed all sorts of things. There was nothing much I could do.

Right then, I noticed a TURBO button on the underside of the right side of the steering column. How had I not seen it before?! Liam was gaining, shooting both pistols once again.

I hit the TURBO button, hoping it would work.

Immediately, we gained fifty MPH, then we climbed up more and more until we were going nearly three hundred MPH. I couldn't breathe. Emma's arms were tight around me, which was good because I was afraid she was going to fly off. I could barely stay in my seat, since there were no seatbelts. I glanced back, my hair flying everywhere from the wind. We were pulling far ahead of Liam. The clouds were just ahead.

We'd reach them in just a few moments.

Then we reached them, and something strange happened. They weren't like typical clouds from back at home. We didn't simply slip into and through them. We busted through them. They were solid, kind of like ice. The ice-type of clouds broke before us, creating a hole in the vast slab of clouds, crumbling to pieces, as we shot through them. The air was colder up here, but brighter.

I could see the top of the mountain.

Within a few moments, Liam broke through the clouds. He wasn't laughing now, however. He was just really, really angry.

7

I could make out the small shack on the top of the mountain. Problem was, it was at least a couple hundred yards away. I didn't think we could make it. I just didn't see how it would be possible. And then it happened. Two of Liam's lasers hit the back of the jet ski.

I didn't see exactly what had happened.

Didn't see the damage that had been done.

But Emma could hold on no longer. She lost her grip and fell off the jet ski. The jet ski was still working, so apparently the lasers hadn't hit anything vital. Unless one of them had hit Emma. Immediately, I spun the small aircraft around in the air to fly towards Emma.

She'd fallen a good twenty feet from me.

Which was coincidental.

Liam was equidistant to her but from the other side.

I couldn't believe the end of this Battle Royale had come down to me vs. Liam—the hacker, the cheater. What could I do? The jet ski was still flying in turbo.

I wouldn't be able to catch Emma going this speed.

Instead, I spiraled just past her, barely missing her, and went straight for Liam. I didn't pull out my gun. Didn't need one. My jet ski was going three hundred MPH and was fronted with steel. Though he had some sort of modded power-up, he wouldn't be able to punch through this.

I plowed directly into him. His body got pinned against the front of my jet ski. I didn't slow, didn't flinch, didn't even blink. Though I was having trouble breathing.

Didn't matter.

I plowed him through the ice clouds, then pulled away, went back up through the opening I'd just created. I saw Emma's body land on the ice clouds, HARD. I was afraid the fall had killed her, but I saw her moving, ever so slightly. I started flying towards her, just over the top of the ice, when Liam plowed through the ice beneath me and plowed into the underside of my jet ski. He launched me upwards; now, I was spinning wildly out of control. I stopped the throttle, trying to get control.

Then I swerved downwards.

He was coming at me again, guns blazing.

This was a good thing: meant he wasn't going to finish off Emma. I glanced past him and saw Emma rolling over. I could clearly see the ice cracking beneath the weight of her body, threatening to fall out from under her.

I grunted. We were so freakin' close for everything to go wrong now.

I needed to get to Emma, but apparently I needed to take care of Liam first.

But how?

He had full power-ups.

That's when I realized. If I could get the wrist bands off of him, this could be a fair fight. Right? Then it would just be Liam vs. Me, but he wouldn't have hacks. How could I get them off of him?

We were about to collide in the sky in the next few seconds.

And that's when the idea hit me.

8

At the last moment, so that he wouldn't expect it, I jumped off the jet ski, right towards him. He was already mid-swing—about to punch through the front of the jet ski. He didn't see me coming. I grabbed onto him in mid-air, which was risky. I held on as tightly as I possibly could. If he threw me off, this was all over. I was gripping him around his neck.

My jet ski flew away without me.

It was just Liam and I in the sky now.

I hoped Emma hadn't fallen through the clouds yet.

I had no way of checking on her.

I was in the fight of my life.

And I needed to get those wristbands off Liam.

He was elbowing me in the side, sending screaming pain through my body. I held on. Then he started flying in circles, trying to throw me off, but he couldn't because I had my arms and legs wrapped around him. He tried shooting me with one of his guns, but I was on his back and he couldn't get the angle right. Then he tried spiraling downwards towards the clouds.

He plowed us directly into the floor of the clouds. They cracked and nearly broke entirely. My body stung with pain and he threw me aside, off of him. I slipped on the icy clouds. But before he could fly away I jumped back on him, reaching for his wrists.

I got ahold of one of the wristbands and yanked it off his hand.

It was weird. I wasn't expecting anything too crazy to happen, but once I removed the wristband, we launched upwards. I accidentally dropped the band. We flew straight up. But he didn't have as much control as he had had, because he was screaming in anger and in fear and we were twisting about wildly, going every direction.

At one point we randomly started going down.

It was all I could do to hold on.

Then we shot upwards once more.

He was trying to control the flight but was having a hard time with only one of the mods.

"Why would you do that?" he roared in anger.

Wasn't it plainly obvious why I would do that?

I laughed a little.

"You're freakin' crazy, Allen!"

I looked up and saw that we were headed towards a very thin bridge. It was made of wooden planks. There were no railings. It was only about two feet wide. If I could get ahold of it, I would feel much safer. The bridge extended from the top of the mountain with the shack on it down to a slightly less tall mountain. It looked sketch, but it was better than trying to hang onto a Liam flying out of control.

We passed the bridge.

I released Liam and let myself fall down to the bridge. I landed on it, but it was so precarious that I fell off. I grabbed the edge of it at the last moment, hung from it. Barely.

Liam shot past me.

But then he started coming back down.

I saw the wristband fall past me.

He'd thrown it off.

Then he landed on the bridge ten feet from me.

This was it then. My plan had slightly worked, though I hadn't been counting on the both of us on a suspension bridge high above the sky. Whichever one of us fell first would die.

I didn't want to fall, nor give him the chance to even attempt to throw me off. I whipped out my pistol and unloaded a full clip on him. All of my bullets broke against him and fell away. He had some kind of shield or power-up that I didn't understand. That's when he whipped out one of his laser guns, dropping to a knee, taking aim at me.

"It's over now, buddy," he said condescendingly.

He was breathing heavy.

He knew I didn't have any ammo left.

No more plays.

Liam smiled nervously. "Thought you had me for a

moment there."

I stood there on the bridge as we swung side to side, ever so slowly. I wasn't moving, was trying to think of some way out of this. I was the leader. I was supposed to have good ideas. I was supposed to be able to handle these kinds of things. My necklace was still blue. I didn't have any incredible ideas or weapons or power-ups or anything.

What could I even do?

"You were a worthy opponent," said Liam. "But you're still a noob."

I smiled right then, right at that moment. I couldn't help myself. Because if there was one thing I wasn't, it was a noob. I'd been working hard my whole life to get good at things, to be better. No matter what others, including my own dad or friends or family had told me, I worked hard.

I was *Allen Diaz* for crying out loud!

My memory came flooding back to me once more. Lots of bad memories, and one of the worst ones: my parents telling me they were going to get a divorce. I remembered sitting on the roof wishing for something more. Because if there was something more, then that would mean that I mattered. In and of myself, I didn't think I mattered much. I knew I did, but I wasn't sure.

It was right then on that bridge that my smile got even wider.

Worthiness is what my necklace read.

I was worthy.

Worthy was a word that meant I was *worth something.*

I knew I was worth something.

I knew it deep, deep down.

But my necklace stayed blue.

That was okay.

I'd figured out how I could beat Liam. The answer was always ME. In a few quick motions, I threw the backpack around to my front, unzipped it, reached inside and pressed the ACTIVATE button on the EMP.

Within the same moment, Liam's gun melted in his hand.

All the metal all around us melted.

I glanced far down and could see Emma, still laying on the ice, but I saw the cracks widen, spreading out, about the break any moment now.

That was the answer.

I'd been training my whole life for this moment. I was enough to beat Liam.

"It's just us now."

"I'm a black belt," Liam said, taking steps towards me.

I took a calming breath. "Well you've never fought me before, have you?"

He smiled, as if he wasn't nervous at all. But I could detect nervousness.

I wasn't nervous at all.

There was ten feet between us.

I was ready to fight.

Only thing was, I had to get this fight over with as fast as possible and somehow get down to Emma.

9

Why my necklace hadn't changed colors, I didn't know. I thought I'd figured it out. Had figured out that I mattered. That I was worthy.

Apparently I was missing something.

I wracked my mind, trying to figure it out as Liam came towards me.

The answer was somewhere in my mind. Had to be. I just couldn't figure it out. Was it something Julie had told me? What had Julie told me? Was it something someone had told me, at any point in my life, ever?

Liam was only a few steps away.

My heart started to sink, because I couldn't figure it

out. I realized that, sure, I had lots of skills, but that didn't mean I was important. Sure, I was a human, but there were billions of humans. I was back to the same dilemma on my rooftop. If there wasn't something more, a higher purpose, then why did I matter?

I looked up into the empty sky, here on Death Island, and I couldn't figure it out. I looked up for the aliens, for God, for anything. For something.

I recalled watching this really old movie on TV called, *The Ten Commandments*. I remembered it had blown my mind how God used Moses to part the Red Sea in two, to turn all the water in Egypt to blood. Moses mattered. God had talked to him through a burning bush.

God had never talked to me through a burning bush.

If God is real, though, I thought to myself, *then I really do matter. Because if God is real that means He made me.* That's when I remembered something I'd learned in Sunday school. Something the teacher had said.

"You are the light of the world."

I am the light of the world.

I'm important in God's eyes.

What if it were true?

Liam was standing before me now and he took a giant swing at me. I dodged backwards. He missed completely. He took another swing. I dodged easily.

Fighting was easy for me.

I was too fast for Liam.

I front kicked him and he flew backwards, landed on his back on the bridge. I took a few steps for him. He was trying to get up. I roundhouse kicked him in the side of the head. He nearly went off the bridge.

"I give up," he said. "Stop!"

But then he got up and tried to kick me.

I grabbed his leg because he'd kicked too slow. I flipped him onto his back. He got up once more, but I side kicked him at an angle, knocking him off the bridge completely.

As he fell away, I was lost in thought.

I needed something.

I needed something more.

I wanted something more.

My life was cool. I had lots of skills, but I wasn't enough. I couldn't see at all, by any stretch of the imagination, that I was worthy or that I mattered.

I looked down, watching Liam fall towards the icy clouds. He was falling fast and it was a long fall so he'd fall through the ice. He'd fall all the way to the ground, to his death.

Which is when I remembered that Emma was down there.

Looking down, I saw she was still there.

Liam would land down within twenty or so feet of her, busting the ice open once and for all. Emma would fall through. I had no devices to fly. No way that I could get her.

I jumped off the bridge anyway, without thinking, with nothing but faith. Faith that something would happen. The wind was rushing past my hair as I dove straight down towards Emma, trying to figure out the mystery. Not able to figure it out. Thinking as hard as I could.

I remembered the old guy, that night my parents had told me about their divorce. He'd told me I was special. Julie had told me I was special. Apparently none of these things mattered.

And that made sense. Because if humans determined

our worth then I only needed to look and listen to my dad to know I wasn't worthy of anything. But I was worth something. Which meant it didn't matter what anyone else thought of me. Only what I thought of myself.

"I matter," I said out loud.

Nothing changed.

I was falling towards Emma.

We were all going to die.

10

Figure it out, Allen, I told myself.

I was falling from the sky—like that meteor I had seen fall onto the Earth. Maybe I mattered because God believed in me. Maybe I was like Moses.

I felt stupid for thinking that.

Moses was obviously a really important person and I was nothing like him. I didn't even have a beard. But then I had a thought. I decided to pray.

"God," I said, loudly, because I really needed help. "Show me that I matter!"

Right then, my necklace turned green.

As I fell towards Emma, I started slowing. It took me a

few seconds to realize it, but I could fly. Right then, Liam hit the ice. It shattered to a million pieces in a wide circle that took Emma with it. Then they were both falling past the clouds and towards the ground.

I completely stopped in the air, floating there, AMAZED.

I felt more powerful, as if I had super strength.

It seemed as though I had the powers Liam had had with the wristbands, except I'd gotten mine fair and square. Well, my team had helped. None of us had gotten the power-up until all of our necklaces had turned green.

You are the light of the world.

"I'm here for a reason. Not just on Death Island. On the planet Earth. God knows me. That's why I matter! He believes in me!"

I smiled larger than ever.

I didn't matter simply because I was Allen Diaz; I mattered simply because I was God's Allen Diaz. Because He had made me, and like Moses He said I was important in this world. *I am the light of this world. We all are. It's just that most of us don't realize it. We're here for a reason, on a mission, to be the light to others and to ourselves.*

Tears came to my eyes as I realized it.

Excited by this new thing I'd finally figured out—it had taken me long enough—I flew down to catch Emma. I flew fast through the hole in the ice. As I flew towards Emma, groups of evil lifeguards flying jet skis were coming towards her. I swooped around in an arc and swiped them all off their jet skies. Easily. I watched Liam continue to fall.

Then I caught Emma in my arms.

With super strength, she was really easy to carry.

I felt like a superhero.

I flew upwards, back through the opening in the clouds.

"Why are you smiling?" asked Emma.

"I figured it out," I said, then I continued smiling, not explaining, simply flying towards the shack at the top of the hill.

I flew Emma to the front door of the shack and set her down. Opening the door, I saw The Professor there, stroking his beard furiously, very nervous. Emma ran towards him and gave him a big hug. He looked genuinely relieved.

Then he looked up at me. "You figured it out, Allen."

He was referring to the necklace.

"You've saved the island."

He went to a computer with Emma and they talked amongst themselves, plugging in calculations. Finally, after about a minute, he turned back. "It's done. It's over."

"What about my team?" I asked.

"You've saved them as well. They'll come back."

"When?"

"Soon," he said.

Then he walked over to me and placed a hand on my shoulder. "I told you you were special," he said. "Didn't I?" I had no clue what he was talking about. "We met once," he said. "Remember?"

At that moment, before I could say anything else, the entire world around me started to fade away. It was as if the molecules were melting away from the very space in which they existed. In only a few moments, the entire world around me was white. Nothing but white.

"Hello?" I asked, genuinely confused.

That's when I remembered—I had met The Professor before. He was the old guy with the dog named Thor who had encouraged me that night I found out my parents were getting a divorce. How did he get onto Death Island?

Suddenly my body laid itself down, on my back, against my will. Then the white faded to black and I fell completely asleep.

It was over.

Just like that.

Epilogue

THE END

I woke up on a bed, in a room that was very white, but not completely white. It was like one of those operating rooms in hospitals, clean and polished and antiseptic. It probably didn't have any germs in it. I was on a bed with an IV in my hand. Looking over I saw three more beds. On the beds were my friends. They were all asleep with IVs in their hands. Gavin, Dev, and Julie.

"Guys," I said.

I sat up and realized I had a massive headache.

Placed a hand to my head.

That's when the one door to the room opened and Petrov stepped in. He was holding a few cans of Coke. I was so confused, rubbing my head.

He handed me a can of Coke. "It helps with the headache," he said.

I accepted it. I was so confused, but it was all starting to fall into place. We'd been put under—put asleep. I saw virtual reality goggles on the table beside me. And suddenly I remembered everything.

We'd been taken into detention, into a normal looking classroom—not that our school was very normal. And we'd been asked to participate in an experiment. We'd signed waivers and were told that our short-term memory would be temporarily wiped so we wouldn't remember what we'd signed up for. Then we'd be put into a game through a state of the art virtual reality rig.

It would feel real, they'd told us.

And it had.

It had felt totally and completely real.

"Congratulations," Petrov said. "I knew you could do it."

I opened the can of Coke. Took a sip.

It tasted great. We must have been on the tables for hours, expending lots of brain energy. I still couldn't believe it. Because Death Island had felt more real than anything I'd experienced.

One by one my friends started waking up, rubbing their headaches away, remembering what had happened and that we'd signed up for the experience.

"That was pretty fun," I said.

"You did it, Allen," Julie said. Then she got up from her bed and walked over to me, taking her IV with her. She gave me a hug. "I knew you could do it."

Suddenly, I felt sad.

I felt sad because I'd thought Death Island was real. Turns out it was a dream after all. I'd kissed Julie in another dream, yet again, and not in real life.

My heart started beating faster in that moment, because I knew what I had to do. And I had to do it right now while Julie was standing beside me. It would be awkward because Petrov was standing right there and Gavin and Dev were waking up right now.

I knew I had to do it, though.

I didn't want to lose what I'd learned on Death Island.

I didn't want to lose Julie.

Not again.

So I grabbed her around the waist and pulled her towards me and kissed her big on the lips. It tasted like Coke and felt just as it had in the Virtual Reality experience on Death Island, except better. She kissed me back. And when we stopped kissing, Dev let out a very lame-sounding holler.

We all laughed.

"So it was real," I said to Julie.

"In a way," she said.

"It certainly was real," said Petrov. "You all learned valuable lessons."

You are the light of the world.

I believed it.

I knew that I mattered.

I realized that it didn't matter what anyone says about me or you. All that matters is that you matter because God made you and loves you.

So dare to dream, kids.

Because you are special.

Like me.